SIR SETH THISTLETHWAITE

Seeks the Truth of Betty the Yeti

Sir Ollie Sir Seth and Shasta

Owl kids

Written by Richard Thake
Illustrated by Vince Chui

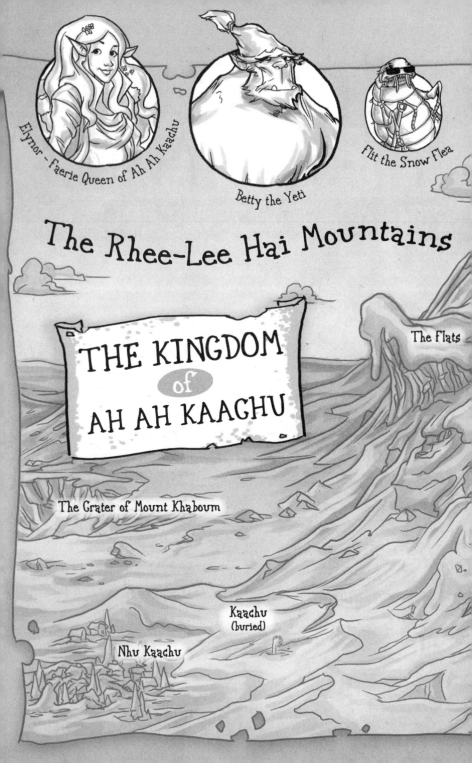

Elynor ~ Faerie Queen of Ah Ah Kaachu

Betty the Yeti

Flit the Snow Flea

The Rhee-Lee Hai Mountains

The Flats

THE KINGDOM of AH AH KAACHU

The Crater of Mount Khaboum

Kaachu
(buried)

Nhu Kaachu

Owlkids Books Inc.
10 Lower Spadina Avenue, Suite 400, Toronto, Ontario M5V 2Z2
www.owlkids.com

Distributed in Canada by University of Toronto Press
5201 Dufferin Street, Toronto, Ontario M3H 5T8

Distributed in the United States by Publishers Group West
1700 Fourth Street, Berkeley, California 94710

Library and Archives Canada Cataloguing in Publication

Thake, Richard, 1938-
    Sir Seth Thistlethwaite seeks the truth of Betty
the yeti / by Richard Thake ; illustrated by Vince Chui.

Issued also in electronic format.
ISBN 978-1-926973-27-2 (bound).--ISBN 978-1-926973-26-5 (pbk.)

    I. Chui, Vince, 1975- II. Title.

PS8639.H36S58 2012   jC813'6   C201

Library of Congress Control Number: 2011935954

Design: Barb Kelly

Canadian Heritage   Patrimoine canadien

Canada

Ontario
Ontario Media Development Corporation

Canada Council for the Arts   Conseil des Arts du Canada

ONTARIO ARTS COUNCIL
CONSEIL DES ARTS DE L'ONTARIO

Société de développement de l'industrie des médias de l'Ontario

We acknowledge the financial support of the Canada Council for the Arts, the Ontario Arts Council, the Government of Canada through the Canada Book Fund (CBF) and the Government of Ontario through the Ontario Media Development Corporation's Book Initiative for our publishing activities.

Manufactured by TC.Transcontinental Gagné
Manufactured in Louiseville, Québec, Canada, in March 2012
Job #47925

A   B   C   D   E   F

Owlkids   Publisher of Chirp, chickaDEE and OWL
www.owlkids.com

CONTENTS

Chapter 1: A Wintry World. 7

Chapter 2: Welcome to Nhu Kaachu 24

Chapter 3: Meet Betty the Yeti 31

Chapter 4: A Nasty, Nail-Gnawing Decision 48

Chapter 5: Sarinda Whind. 53

Chapter 6: Who's in the Hole? 59

Chapter 7: In the Midst of the Mids 73

Chapter 8: Elynor Makes a Discovery. 82

Chapter 9: Rumbling? What Rumbling? 87

Chapter 10: Yackety's Advice. 96

Chapter 11: The Great Wall of Ollie. 101

Chapter 12: Sir Seth Thwacks & Thwarts the Thing . .110

Chapter 13: Flit's Super Surprise 122

Chapter 14: A Race to the Finish! 129

Chapter 15: Poor Old Nhu Kaachu. 135

Epilogue: The Mists of Moro. 147

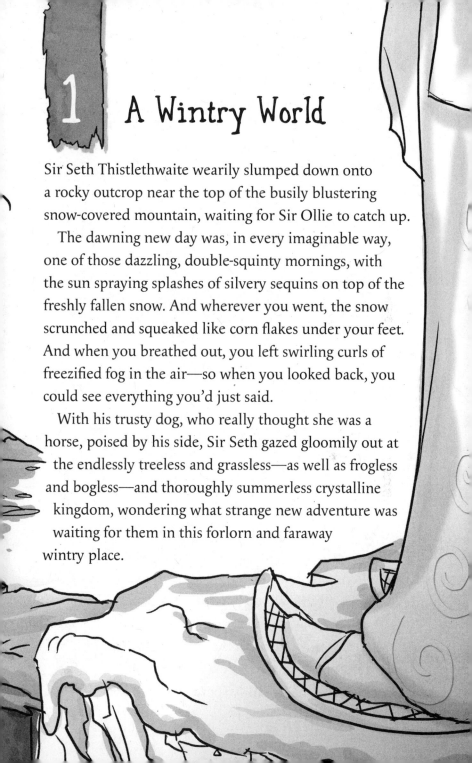

1 A Wintry World

Sir Seth Thistlethwaite wearily slumped down onto
a rocky outcrop near the top of the busily blustering
snow-covered mountain, waiting for Sir Ollie to catch up.

The dawning new day was, in every imaginable way,
one of those dazzling, double-squinty mornings, with
the sun spraying splashes of silvery sequins on top of the
freshly fallen snow. And wherever you went, the snow
scrunched and squeaked like corn flakes under your feet.
And when you breathed out, you left swirling curls of
freezified fog in the air—so when you looked back, you
could see everything you'd just said.

With his trusty dog, who really thought she was a
horse, poised by his side, Sir Seth gazed gloomily out at
the endlessly treeless and grassless—as well as frogless
and bogless—and thoroughly summerless crystalline
kingdom, wondering what strange new adventure was
waiting for them in this forlorn and faraway
wintry place.

He straightened the pot that he'd got from under the sink, which he thought was much, much better as a Mighty Knight's helmet than it ever was as a pot.

"By golly, Shasta," he sighed, completely overwhelmed, "I've never seen so much nothing as all this. We're never gonna find anyone up here."

Then, just as he was about to continue wending his way farther up the mountain, from nowhere, Sir Seth heard a tinkling, little-girl voice say:

"Perhaps I can help you."

Sir Seth was so shocked, he nearly jumped right out of his woolly white socks and knee-high silver boots—just like the knights of yore always wore wherever they went, whenever they went there. He whirled, and with his trusty sword at the ready, came nose to nose...with somebody's knees.

"Uh, hello," he managed to mutter as he began to look up. Then up. And up. Then up and up some more. Until he couldn't look up any farther without falling over.

"What are you doing up here in Ah Ah Kaachu—all by yourself?" the soft, unusual voice continued. "You must be either seriously delirious or decidedly lost. Even on a frightfully delightful sunshiny day such as this, nobody ever comes all the way up here to Ah Ah Kaachu...unless, for some reason, they feel that they must."

Her face was sheltered in the shifting shadows of her white fur-lined hood, which made it difficult for Sir Seth to see her...but he instantly sensed she had the calm, gentle air of a stately young lady with dark, almond-shaped eyes, framed by flowing cascades of long, snowy-white hair.

As he continued to squint up at his most unusual host, he also noticed she was dressed completely in white. And was surrounded by a halo of soft white light glowing all around her like lightly falling snow. There was even a little white mouse sitting on one of her shoulders.

Then she threw back the large, floppy hood of her white fleece-lined parka and turned toward the sun. And for the first time, Sir Seth saw her face clearly, without shadows. And the minute he did, he gasped right out loud. Then he took another look and double-gasped twice as right-out-loud as the gasp before that. Whoever she was, she was so utterly lovely, even Shasta was speechless.

Not only was she double-gulp beautiful, she was more breathtakingly beautiful even than that. There was also a quiet majesty about her that suggested she was much, much more than just an ordinary seven-foot-tall elf. But Sir Seth couldn't imagine just what that might be.

"Uh, did you say this is Ah Ah Kaachu?" he finally managed to mutter.

"Yes," she smiled warmly. "Welcome to Ah Ah Kaachu. This is indeed a rare pleasure. Not many visitors come all the way up here."

"I don't blame them," Sir Seth smiled, shielding his eyes from the sun. "But um...who are you? And what are you doing up here all by yourself?"

"I've come here to put a stop to all the avalanches..."

"Avalanches?!" Sir Seth shuddered, taking two steps back. "What avalanches?"

"Oh, don't worry," she continued reassuringly. "Before an avalanche comes, the mountain gives you lots and lots of warning rumbles and grumbles."

Sir Seth looked up to the top of the windswept mountain. "Good. Because there sure is a lot of snow up there."

"My name is Elynor," she said simply, holding out her hand. "And you are..."

"Sir Seth Thistlethwaite of the Mighty Knights of Right & Honor, at your service, my lady," he said with a gallant bow and a sweep of one hand. "And that's my faithful steed, Shasta, over there," he said, pointing to the golden retriever who was excitedly romping around in the snow. "And somewhere out there is my friend, Sir Ollie Everghettz..."

"SirOlliewillbehereinaminute," came a speedy Squeakspeak reply from the little mouse on Elynor's shoulder. "He'sgothisfoottangledupinasnagglefootbush."

"Jabberjaws!" Sir Seth said with a smile. "Good to see you again!"

"Oh, of course," Elynor quickly said. "You've already met my friend, the messenger of the Ice Mice."

"Hi. Goodtoseeyou,too," the little mouse greeted him in its tongue-tangling Squeakspeak. "Thesearetheknights we'vebeenseeking,myQueen. ShallIgoandtellthevillage?"

"Yes," Elynor sighed with relief. "Please go and tell the others that we have found the Mighty Knights at long last."

As the little mouse quickly jumped down and disappeared, a huge sunny smile brightened Elynor again. "Oh, sir knight, this is indeed a deliriously delicious delight! We truly have been looking everywhere for you."

Sir Seth straightened shyly and brushed some snow from his sleeve. "Uh, did I hear Jabberjaws right? Are you really a queen?"

11

"Why yes." Elynor nodded modestly. "I am the Faerie Queen of all Ah Ah Kaachu."

"My Queen!" Sir Seth said with a low, snowy bow. "Jabberjaws said you need our help. How may we serve you?"

"We need you to rid us of Betty the Yeti...before she kills us all."

Shasta stopped dead in the middle of a sniff and looked up.

"Kills you?" Sir Seth gasped, gaping at Elynor as though she had just hit him on his thumb with a hammer. "Why does she want to do that?"

"Nobody knows for sure." Elynor shuddered all over just thinking about it. "That's why we've been trying to find you—you must help us, Sir Seth, before she buries Nhu Kaachu."

Sir Seth looked up the mountain. "I didn't know yetis did yucky things like that."

"Oh, indeed, they do," she said with another shudder. "You won't find a yeti any yuckier than Betty. She's as yettishly yucky as yucky ever gets."

But much to Elynor's surprise, Sir Seth seemed to be excited about meeting a yeti. "Yeah?" he replied. "What makes you so sure it's Betty? I thought avalanches just sorta happened."

"Not around here!" she said, pointing up the mountain. "See that gigantic ridge of snow up there? Well, Betty has been sending down snowslides—or feeders—to fill up The Flats for a long, long time now..."

Sir Seth shielded his eyes from the sun. "The Flats? What are The Flats?"

"Well...you can't see them from down here," Elynor explained, "but it's a large flat area near the top of the mountain. And every time Betty sends another new feeder down, the pile of snow on The Flats keeps getting larger and larger. Eventually, there'll be so much snow The Flats will overflow—and there'll be an avalanche SO BIG, it'll be the biggest avalanche there's ever been. At any time! Ever!"

Then, just as though the snow had been listening in, the mountain suddenly rumbled and grumbled beneath their feet. Shasta ran behind Sir Seth and nervously peeped out between his legs.

"Whoa! What's that?" he gasped, wide-eyed with wonder.

Elynor pointed to the top of the mountain. "It must be Betty sending another feeder down onto The Flats. You can just see the snow now..."

Sir Seth looked up and if he squinted, he could just barely make out a cloudy cascade of tumbling, rumbling snow that shook the mountain as it slowly thundered down toward The Flats.

"By golly," he uttered in awe. "If all that snow comes down here, we'll be..." But he couldn't find the words to finish his worrying.

"Buried forever," Elynor finished Sir Seth's sentence for him, looking uncomfortably down at him for a long, long, long time. "Perhaps now you believe me, Sir Seth. Betty is much more evil and awful, by far, than anything you've ever met anywhere else in all your knightly travels. Kaachu folklore is filled with many, many terrifying tales about Betty that are so awfully eerie and so frightfully feary you can't even begin to believe what they say."

Sir Seth stared at her nervously. "Yeah? Like what?"

Elynor leaned closer. "Well, one day, ten years ago, she suddenly swooped down and attacked the school in the village of Kaachu. Then, the very next day, she sent an avalanche crashing down the mountain and buried the entire village. And now, she's getting ready to do the same thing all over again to the village of Nhu Kaachu."

Sir Seth was shocked all the way down to his size-six white socks. "She buried a whole village? Why did she do that?"

"Nobody knows." Elynor shrugged. "Yetis are just like that, I guess."

Sir Seth shuddered all over, still thinking about the village. No wonder Elynor wanted the Mighty Knights to help her.

"That's worse than having a tooth filled without freezing it first! What does she look like?"

Elynor shuddered, too. "Well, I've never actually seen her myself, but the stories all say she's at least ten feet tall and so totally, totally terrifyingly frightful that if you sneak just one peek, you'll scream for a week without taking a breath."

Sir Seth gasped at the thought. "A whole week? All on one breath?"

Elynor leaned even closer. "Yes! But even worse than that, if you look at Betty for more than a minute, you'll become so rigidly, frigidly frozen with fear, you won't be able to eat for at least eleventeen hours or more."

Sir Seth's mouth fell open in chattering, clattering shock at the unblinkingly unthinkable thought of...

"Nothing at all?" Seth gasped. "That's more frightening than being hit twice by lightning. I'm glad Sir Ollie wasn't here to hear that!"

He immediately looked down the mountain for his friend. "I wonder what's taking him so long?"

"A snagglefoot bush takes a long time to untangle." Elynor smiled. "Your friend will be here soon..."

Sir Seth looked back up the mountain at the ominous ridge of snow. Then, with a flourish, he threw back his cape and drew his sword, holding it high. "And when he does, no matter how hairy and scary this Betty may be, I assure you the Mighty Knights won't let you down. So tell me, my lady...where does Betty the Yeti live?"

Elynor hesitated, then pointed the rest of the way up to the absolute snowiest, blowiest, tippiest top of the Rhee-Lee Hai Mountains. "Betty lives way up there at the very top where the snow touches the sky, on the mountain without any name."

"No name?" Sir Seth repeated. "That's kinda strange. I thought that all mountains had names."

"Yes, it is rather odd," Elynor agreed, as though thinking about it for the first time. "I guess no one in Ah Ah Kaachu has ever done anything to have the mountain named after them."

Sir Seth paused for a moment, deep in thought. "Um, do you mind if I ask you a personal question..."

Elynor shrugged. "No, not at all. What would you like to know?"

"Well, I've never met anyone like you before. You're, uh, sorta too short to be a giant and too nice to be an ogre and too tall to be an elf. So, uh, what are you?"

Elynor pulled herself up proudly. "Oh, I am absolutely, positively an elf. In fact, I'm a very, very rare snowshoe elf." She glowed, showing Sir Seth one of her size-sixty-six snowshoe-shaped feet. "See? I have snowshoes for feet.

And as far as I know, there's just me and my father and mother and my sixty sisters and thirty-three brothers— and one or two others—who have snowshoes for feet, and stand seven feet tall in their socks. But as you can see, snowshoes come in handy in all of this snow."

"I've never heard of a snowshoe elf," Sir Seth said with surprise. "And come to think of it, I didn't even know there were lady elves."

Elynor stared at Sir Seth with surprise. "Of course there are lady elves, silly," she huffed a white puff of freezified fog with an indignant sort of a snort. "If you take a look all around you, you'll see there are lady and gentleman everythings. There are lady and gentleman bees and fleas and trees and chickadees. As well as lady and gentleman hedgehogs and bulldogs and bullfrogs and prairie dogs...and lady and gentleman snakes and lakes and snowflakes. As well as the Himalayan and the Hermalayan Mountains. I thought everyone, everywhere, knew that."

Sir Seth had never even thought of a thought like that before.

"No, I didn't know that. But aren't you too tall to be an elf?" Sir Seth argued. "I sorta thought elves only stood as tall as small trees."

"Oh, no." Elynor smiled her sunny white smile. "There are many, many kinds of elves. There are tall elves and small elves and barn elves and snowy elves and tawny elves and scrawny elves and brawny elves and twelve kinds of elves-that-you've-never-heard-of-before elves."

"Yeah, Sir Seth, even I knew that," a familiar voice interrupted them.

Elynor whirled to see who it was. "Goodness me, two visitors! Both on the same day. You must be Sir Ollie. Welcome to Ah Ah Kaachu, sir knight," she beamed with instant delight. "I am Elynor, the Faerie Queen of Ah Ah Kaachu."

"At your service, my lady," Sir Ollie said with a polite knightly bow. "Here to help you however I can..."

Suddenly, Shasta, who had been busily burrowing into the snow, began woofing and whining excitedly the way most dogs do when they forget they're supposed to be acting like horses.

"What have you found, girl?" Sir Seth said, slowly making his way through the waist-deep snow.

When he reached Shasta, Sir Seth stopped dead in his tracks. Then jumped back in shock.

It was a hand! With a long claw-like finger pointing straight at him.

"Caw! Caw! Caw! Caw!" Sir Seth sent out the Mighty Knights' secret Four-Caw Alert over one shoulder. "Oll... Oll...Ollie! Come here! Quick!"

"Quick? It's impossible to do anything quickly up here," he shouted back. "This freezing, sneezing snow's so deep, it's almost up to my nose."

Sir Seth couldn't take his eyes off that accusing finger

pointing right at him. "Ollie, hurry! We have a full Four-Caw Alert!"

Sir Ollie stopped dead in his tracks. "Four caws?"

Immediately, Sir Ollie remembered that four caws is the number of caws crows use to warn the rest of the flock that an intruder is entering the fields. So, to a Mighty Knight of Right & Honor, a Four-Caw Alert is something so seriously solemn, it needs four "really's" to really explain it. Imagine that summer holidays had been canceled. Or the bubble gum factory had suddenly blown up. That's a Four-Caw Alert.

When Elynor heard that Shasta had dug up a hand, she immediately stooped and scooped up Sir Ollie under one arm and with her snowshoe-sized feet, she reached Sir Seth's side in about three super-sized strides. Then, putting Sir Ollie down, the three of them and Shasta stood there, all staring at the claw-like hand in the snow.

"Don't touch it!"
Sir Ollie warned everyone.

"It's probably all covered in germs. You could get double diphtheria—and die!"

"What's a hand doing here in the middle of...nothing?" Sir Seth wondered out loud, looking at the bleak emptiness all around them.

Elynor knelt down and carefully began brushing the snow away. "I know this hand."

"You do?"

She took a deep breath. "Yes. It is the hand of the statue of the town crier. When the first village of Kaachu was still here, it was the town crier's main job to tell the people when an avalanche was coming. Then, on that awful and unforgettable morning, without any warning— an avalanche did come thundering down the mountain and in one nightmarish minute, it buried the village and everything in it."

Ollie looked up at Elynor. "Everything?"

"Yes," Elynor said slowly. "Every house, every mouse, every tree, every flea, every worm, germ, and bee. Everything. And to this day, the people all say it was Betty who caused it."

"What about the...people in the town?" Sir Seth asked, almost afraid to find out. "What happened to them?"

"They got away just in time," Elynor said with a sigh. "Then they built the village of Nhu Kaachu beyond that hill way over there, far enough from the mountain that they felt it was safe."

"But...why would Betty want to do something like that

to the village?" Sir Ollie wondered out loud.

"I don't know," Elynor sighed sadly. "There can't be any good reason." She looked directly at Sir Seth and shrugged. "Can there?"

All Sir Seth could do was shrug, too. "No. Not that I can think of."

But for some inside-his-heart reason, Sir Seth couldn't believe that even a yeti would bury a whole village for no reason. And he didn't know why. Which was rather strange, because he'd never met Betty. Or any other yeti, for that matter.

Sir Seth looked up at Elynor. "How do you know it was Betty?"

Elynor sat down and offered Sir Seth and Sir Ollie a handful of snow. "Well, that's a very, very sorry and folklorey story—that grows a little longer each time it's retold. The last time I heard it, it took about twelve and a half minutes to tell. But if you're in no hurry to go, why don't we sit down and share a handful of snow? And I'll tell you everything I know."

"Snow?" Sir Ollie asked, looking up at Elynor.

"Yes, snow. Didn't you know? Kaachuian snow is magic. Here, quick, take a lick, then close your eyes and you'll see...it tastes like lemon meringue pie. Or anything else you want it to be."

Sir Ollie immediately brightened. "Anything?"

"Yes. And sharing snow is the way we Kaachuians enter into each other's minds—which makes it impossible for a

Kaachuian to tell a lie." She took a slow lick. "Mmmmm, fresh-picked strawberries. My favorite. Try it."

Sir Seth took a quick lick. "Hey, you're right. It's magic! Mine tastes like red and green jellybeans. But please...tell us more about Betty!"

"Yeah, you said Betty started the avalanche," Sir Ollie said eagerly, taking a long luxurious lick of his double-decker, double-chocolate, banana-butterscotch double-dip ice-cream handful of snow topped with six scoops of whipped cream and two cherries. "How do you know it was Betty?"

Elynor shrugged. "It couldn't be anyone else. Betty lives up there, all by herself."

Sir Seth took another long slow lick of snow and looked up at Elynor. As he did, he suddenly sensed a strong feeling of closeness and trust between them, as though he was somehow entering Elynor's mind. Except that Sir Ollie

was enjoying his magical ice cream sundae sooooo much he was drowning out most of Elynor's thoughts.

"So," he continued, "what happened the day that Betty attacked the school..."

"Well, instead of me telling you," Elynor said, standing up, "let's go down to Nhu Kaachu and talk to Miss Laurie-Lee Lerner. She's the teacher who was there that awful day ten years ago. She can tell you everything that happened. Nhu Kaachu is just beyond those tall fir trees on the other side of that big hill over there."

"Good idea. Let's go," Sir Ollie said, getting to his feet.

"Follow me," Elynor smiled, looking down at Sir Seth. "You can walk in my footsteps."

Elynor turned and led the way to the village. But she already knew that deep down in his heart, Sir Seth still wasn't sure Betty was the real problem at all. Their sharing of the snow had secretly told her so.

Welcome to Nhu Kaachu

Sir Seth, Sir Ollie, and Shasta waded through the knee-deep snow, following in Elynor's size-sixty-six footsteps until they reached the top of a hill. There, nestled up against a frilly forest of fir at the foot of the unnamed mountain, was the quaint little village of Nhu Kaachu.

Everything seemed so peacefully perfect and quiet and calm, it was hard to believe Betty wanted to bury it all under ten billion tons of snow.

"Ah, here comes the mayor of Nhu Kaachu to greet us," Elynor pointed out. "Mayor Mae Knott can tell you all about the day that Betty attacked the school."

"Indeed I can!" Mayor Knott greeted them warmly. "Welcome, welcome. You must be the Mighty Knights of Right & Honor—and this must be your trusty horse, Shasta. Thank you for coming here to help us."

Sir Seth bowed deeply. "It's our Mighty Knightly duty, your mayorship, to go wherever we must..."

"To seek out all that's wrong in the world and make everything right!" Sir Ollie finished the Mighty Knights' Promise with a bow of his own.

"And I'm sure you shall!" Mayor Mae Knott smiled. "Now come along. If you want to hear about Betty, you must meet Miss Laurie-Lee Lerner. She's the school teacher at Nhu Kaachu Public School Number Two. She was there the day Betty first appeared."

As the Mighty Knights walked toward the school, the villagers stopped in the street and pointed to them with excited smiles and called out...

"All hail the Mighty Knights!"

"Thank you for coming here to help us get rid of Betty!"

"Nobody likes Betty much, do they?" asked Sir Ollie.

"Can you blame them?" Sir Seth said softly. "But I still don't understand why Betty wants to be so awful."

As the Mayor Mae Knott led them into Nhu Kaachu Public School Number Two, Miss Laurie-Lee Lerner got up from her desk and walked primly to greet them.

"Ah, Sir Seth and Sir Oliver. Thank you for coming here to help us," she stated. "However, it's quite clear that Nhu Kaachu is now rather safe, with the hill to protect us."

"Safe? You don't know what Betty's planning to do!" Elynor interrupted. "She's building an avalanche so HUNORMOUSLY BIG, it will spill over the hill like a tsunami of snow—and bury the village just like before."

Miss Lerner looked at Elynor in utter surprise. "Oh no, no, no, dear. We're so far from the mountain now. There's not that much snow in all of Ah Ah Kaachu."

"Yes, there is," Elynor interrupted. "I've seen the snow building up on The Flats. We're not ready for Betty."

"Uh, speaking of Betty," Sir Seth said, taking a seat at one of the desks, "could you tell us what happened the day she came to the school?"

Miss Lerner took a deep breath and sat down, too. "Well, ten years ago, I was the new grade two teacher. I remember it well. At precisely one minute to nine, the big brass bell at the tip of the steeple began its singsong dinging and donging, announcing the first day of school. How absolutely, splendidly fine. Because when the bell stopped ringing, the time would be exactly *no* minutes to nine. On the dot. On the spot. Which of course meant that anybody arriving any later than that would be unacceptably, inexcusably…"

Miss Lerner let this last word hang in the air, her eyebrow arched in anticipation.

"Uh—late?" Sir Ollie guessed.

"Yes! Late! Very good." Miss Lerner nodded with an approving smile. "I practice precision and perfection in all that I do. Which isn't always easy to do. Especially in a village as slow and sleepy as snowy Kaachu was.

"Then! At exactly one minute past nine, there came an ominously, thunderously rumbling and frighteningly grumbling roar from somewhere outside. I immediately put down my pen and walked quickly over to the open schoolroom door and looked out and looked up.

"And there, much to my shock and knee-knocking chagrin, an out-of-control avalanche was thundering down the side of the mountain, straight for the school!

"However, upon more thorough and thoughtful inspection, I noticed that this most peculiar avalanche wasn't heading *straight* for the school. In fact, it looked a lot like an extra-large icicle. And didn't seem to be heading in a straight line to anywhere at all. Spraying a sky-high rooster-tail of fresh, sequined snow, this odd and unusual icicle was bent and intent on careening crazily from the east side of the mountain all the way to the west before changing its mind and schussing and schlossing its wild way all the way back to the east—while writing the letter 'S' at least ten times in the snow wherever it went.

"Before I could do anything, this strange sky-high snowball rumbled and tumbled right up to the front door, blew me easily out of the way, and deposited a most frightful, unforgettable sight—a ten-foot-tall yeti—right in the middle of the room in the middle of the school.

"'OH NO! IT'S KING KONG!' the entire class all screamed in one shrill and utterly terrified, scarified voice. 'PLEASE, MISS LERNER! WE'RE ALL GOING TO DIE! SAVE US! DO SOMETHING, QUICK!'"

By now, Miss Lerner had stood up, acting out the scene almost as she would for her class.

"Then they all took one more look and screamed so loud and so high that only dogs and frogs could hear it.

'HELP! IT'S AN AWFUL, YUCKY YETI...

QUICK! CALL THE POLICE!

CALL ANYONE AT ALL!

"It was utterly stutteringly toe-tinglingly terrifying! And that's about all I can recall," Miss Lerner sighed, exhausted, and sat back in her seat.

"And, uh, what happened to Betty?" Sir Seth asked.

Miss Laurie-Lee Lerner looked puzzled at first. "Hmmmm, I really don't know," she had to admit. "All we know is...she went back up to the top of the mountain and a few days later, an avalanche came crashing down and buried the entire village."

Sir Seth turned to Sir Ollie. "By golly, Sir Ollie, I think the Mighty Knights should go up there and teach Betty the Yeti some manners."

"Right you are, Sir Seth. The time for talk is over. It's time for action instead!" He automatically reached for El Gonzo, his sword. But he forgot that El Gonzo was gonzo! "My trusty sword! It got all burned up by that awful ogre Ooz! Now what am I gonna do?"

"Going up the mountain without a sword?" the mayor gasped. "What a doubly dangerous thing to do!"

"Yes, ma'am, indeed it is!" Sir Ollie said. "But someone must go up there and stop Betty!"

"Then you had best take the Ancient Sword of Kaachu," she said, turning to her assistant. "Please fetch my father's sword for Sir Ollie."

"Your father's ancient sword?" Sir Ollie double-gulped all over again. "What an honor! Do you mind if I call it 'El Gonzo' just like my old one?"

Mayor Knott smiled proudly. "Please do. My father would be honored that you are using his battle sword to protect Ah Ah Kaachu."

The messenger handed the sword to Sir Ollie, who held it reverently and swished a figure eight in the cold air. It was the most exciting moment in Sir Ollie's entire Mighty Knightly life. "A *for-real* Kaachuian battle sword," Sir Ollie *ooohhhed* in awe. "Oh, Sir Seth, isn't it triple-cool times ten?"

"Humphhh," Sir Seth sniffed, sorta miffed. "Looks just like an old broomstick to me."

"Yeah? Well, not if you squint real hard..."

"C'mon," Sir Seth said anxiously. "Let's ride!"

Sir Ollie swished his new sword in the air again. "Right! And do what we came here to do!"

Meet Betty the Yeti

With brightly colored pennants blowing in the brisk mountain breeze, Sir Seth hoisted his lance high over his head. "Lances at the ready!" he called over one shoulder. "Forward ho, Mighty Knights! To victory we go!"

Sir Ollie lifted his lance to the "On Guard" position and looked up the mountain. "Yo! I'm with you all the way...but, wow, it sure is a long way to go, isn't it?"

Elynor smiled back at him. "So it's a good thing you're a Mighty Knight, right?"

"Yeah, right. I was just gonna say that." He grinned sheepishly.

And so—slowly but surely—the little expedition began to make its magnificent way up the side of the towering, snow-covered mountain. A snowshoe elf. Two Mighty Knights. And a big old smiley dog that thought it was a horse.

Still, they trekked tirelessly ever onward and upward, inching their way to the remotest and loneliest parts of the mountain. And as they climbed higher and higher, Sir Seth found himself looking down on a huge snow-covered plain that stretched for miles in front of them— The Flats.

He tugged the bottom of Elynor's long white coat. "Time to take a break." He puffed clouds of frilly frost, trying to catch his breath in the thinning air.

"Oh dear, yes," she instantly agreed, sitting down beside him. "I'm sorry. I forgot you're not used to the thin air up here."

"Uh...could I ask you a question?" Sir Ollie sighed, as he sat down beside them.

"Of course. What would you like to know?" Elynor smiled.

"From up here, I can see how those feeders have been building up and building up on The Flats. So how come some of the villagers aren't worried about that?"

Elynor shrugged. "Because none of them have been up here to see how BIG the avalanche is really going to be."

Sir Seth stood up. "Well, all it's gonna take is one more big feeder and there'll be an avalanche so HUMONGOUSLY GINORMOUS, it'll last for a month and six days!"

Elynor looked back down onto The Flats. "You're right. It really is much, much worse than I feared..."

Sir Ollie paused, looking up. "Um, has anybody

thought about what'll happen to us if one of those feeders starts coming down here right now?"

Both Mighty Knights immediately double-gulped and looked up to Elynor for an answer.

"We can only hope that doesn't happen," she said nervously, looking up to the top of the mountain. "Hurry, we must keep going."

They continued to climb up, up, up into the cold thinning air, until Sir Seth finally slumped down beside Shasta to catch his breath and noticed a dark slitty opening up near the top of the mountain that looked like it could be the mouth of a cave.

He tapped Elynor on the back of her knee. "See that dark hole waaaay up there? What's that?"

"Um...I'm not sure," she had to admit. "It looks like a cave."

"Y'mean, you don't know what it is?"

Elynor blushed brightly. "Well, no. I've never been this far up the mountain before. Nobody has. Kaachuians don't dare come up here

because everyone's afraid of what Betty might do if we did."

Sir Seth fell back flat in the snow. "Well, how are we supposed to stop Betty if we don't even know where she lives?"

"Oh, she's up there somewhere," Elynor assured him quickly. "No doubt about that—this is definitely yeti territory."

Sir Seth wasn't so sure. "Well, if you've never been up there before, how do you know what's there? There could be all kinds of ogres and uggers and cavemen and stuff...and maybe no yetis at all."

But before Elynor could answer, Sir Ollie interrupted their thoughts with an urgent: "Caw! Caw! Caw! Caw!"

Uh oh. Another full Four-Caw Alert!

Sir Seth immediately took a tighter grip on his lance and tensed for action. "What's up, Sir Ollie?"

"Listen! Can you hear a sorta screeching noise?" he said, cocking his head. "It sounds like someone's scraping their fingernails on a blackboard somewhere."

Even Shasta stopped sniffing the snow and perked up.

"Look! Up there!" Sir Seth

34

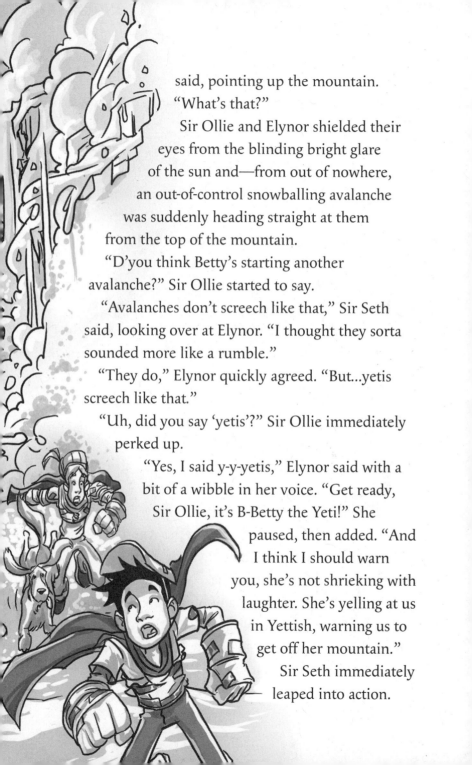

said, pointing up the mountain. "What's that?"

Sir Ollie and Elynor shielded their eyes from the blinding bright glare of the sun and—from out of nowhere, an out-of-control snowballing avalanche was suddenly heading straight at them from the top of the mountain.

"D'you think Betty's starting another avalanche?" Sir Ollie started to say.

"Avalanches don't screech like that," Sir Seth said, looking over at Elynor. "I thought they sorta sounded more like a rumble."

"They do," Elynor quickly agreed. "But...yetis screech like that."

"Uh, did you say 'yetis'?" Sir Ollie immediately perked up.

"Yes, I said y-y-yetis," Elynor said with a bit of a wibble in her voice. "Get ready, Sir Ollie, it's B-Betty the Yeti!" She paused, then added. "And I think I should warn you, she's not shrieking with laughter. She's yelling at us in Yettish, warning us to get off her mountain."

Sir Seth immediately leaped into action.

"Spread out!" he said decisively as he lowered his lance to Position Number One, ready to charge. "Prepare to defend Lady Elynor!"

"Lance lowered and ready," Sir Ollie confirmed, moving to the right.

"Rrrrruff," Shasta confirmed, edging over to the left.

Then the four of them stood there and watched in open-mouthed awe as the high-tailed "avalanche" schussed and sloshed down the mountain at almost warp speed, slewing and corkscrewing and zigging and zagging wildly as it hissed across the crisp icy snow.

"Hey, y'know, too bad it's Betty. That sorta looks like fun," Sir Ollie couldn't help saying. "What kind of sled is that?"

"It looks like a giant rocket sled," Sir Seth drooled. "Wow, how cool is that!"

"Too cool to be true!" Sir Ollie drooled back.

"It's an icicle," Elynor interrupted all the dribbling and drooling. "Betty calls it her 'Icicle Built for Two.'"

"For two? Who else lives up there?"

Elynor didn't take her eyes from the schussing sled. "Well, the stories all say Betty lives up there with a shaggy Yubetan yak, called Yackety."

But before she could say anything more, the icy sled suddenly hissed to a stop right beside them. And sitting there, staring back at them staring back at her, was an actual, factual, irate, hairy-faced, scary-faced, gigantic white yeti in a crash helmet carved from the vee of a

Kaachuian snowball tree and dark goggles made from tightly stretched snowhoppers' knees.

Now, as you can easily guess, any yeti is a frightening sight that you really don't want to see, but an irate yellow-eyed yeti is at least ten times more unwanted than that. Even Shasta scurried behind Sir Seth and growled out from between the knight's legs.

Betty the Yeti silently glared at all four of them as she slowly slid off her sled and stood up until she was fully ten fearsome feet tall. First, she glowered at Elynor, then glared down at the two Mighty Knights with her freezifying slitty little yellow yeti eyes. What appeared to be vampire-bat venom oozed out of both sides of a nightmarish, knight-gnawing, fanged, cavernous mouth filled with thousands of slimy strings of things that you find inside pumpkins and which were forming frosty puddles of green slime and sludge around both of her long, pointy-clawed feet.

Then she slowly, wordlessly, raised one of her huge hairy white arms and pointed down the mountain with a long, broken-nailed finger, and in a deep, menacing voice that sounded like a herd of hippos galloping down a small hallway together, issued the following four-word warning:

"Get. Off. My. Mountain."

For the briefest snick of a teeny micro-minute, Sir Seth was so suddenly knee-knockingly nervous he completely forgot that he was a fearless Mighty Knight. He just stood there, staring at those terrifying yellow tiger-like eyes and gnashing, knight-gnawing teeth. Beside him, Sir Ollie started to reach for El Gonzo, but for once, his arm was smarter than his mind was—and rigidly refused to budge.

Nobody moved.

So Betty repeated her warning, this time in a voice that sounded like ninety-nine rhinos stomping on a tin roof.

"I SAID...GET! OFF! MY! MOUNTAIN!"

Elynor suddenly stepped in front of the two knights with both hands on her hips. It was the first time Sir Seth had seen her so upset. "Your mountain? This is everybody's mountain, Betty! Why must you be so evil and awful and...and so beastly!"

Betty leaned down until her nose was two inches from Elynor's. "AND JUST WHO ARE YOU?"

"Um, I am E-Elynor...," she started to stutter.

Suddenly aroused and irate, Sir Ollie immediately jumped to Elynor's aid. "Yeah. And in case you didn't know, she's the Faerie Queen of all Ah Ah Kaachu."

"Including this mountain," Sir Seth added on to Sir Ollie's add-on.

"The Queen?" Betty sneered with disdain. "Well, you might be the queen of the bottom of the mountain, but I'm the queen of the top!" She glared down at Elynor with her yellow-eyed glower and growled, "Now, for the last time, I'm warning you...get off my mountain!"

"NO! Not until you stop filling up The Flats with all those feeders!" Sir Seth snorted with sudden Mighty Knightly courage.

"Yeah!" Sir Ollie blurted out almost as bravely. "That avalanche will bury Nhu Kaachu forever and ever! Why would you want to do something like that?"

But instead of making her angrier, the two Mighty Knights had caught Betty completely by surprise. "Feeders? Flats? I've never heard of them!" she grunted grumpily, looking warily from one to the other.

"You know exactly what we're talking about!" Elynor almost shouted. "We're talking about the snow you've been building up on The Flats..."

"Me?" Betty said, pointing to herself. "Do you think I'm doing that?"

"YES! WE DO!" Elynor and Sir Seth and Sir Ollie and Shasta all shouted at once.

Betty roared with yellowy stringy-thinged laughter. "HAH! You don't want me. You want The Hole Thing!"

"The what?" Elynor and Sir Seth and Sir Ollie and Shasta all shouted all over again.

Betty leaned closer. "I said...The Hole Thing."

"Uh, what's that?"

"Just what its name says...it's a Thing that lives in The Hole at the top of the mountain," Betty bellowed. "And The Hole Thing is the whole problem around here. Not me! But whenever I try to tell anyone that, no one will listen."

"Oh, snow feathers! There's no such thing as a Hole Thing—and you know it!" Elynor scoffed, convinced that Betty was making the whole Hole Thing thing up.

"You call yourself the Faerie Queen of Ah Ah Kaachu— and you've never heard of The Hole Thing?" Betty scoffed right back. "HAH! Some queen you are!"

Elynor angrily turned to the two knights. "We're wasting time! Betty's making up this entire Hole Thing story so no one will blame her for creating the avalanches!"

Betty narrowed her eyes. "Well, your majesty, if you don't believe me, then why don't you go up there and find out for yourself!" Betty dared, then added, "You're not afraid of some silly old killer caterpillar, are you?"

"K-k-killer caterpillar?" Sir Ollie immediately echoed nervously.

"Yes," Betty sniffed. "That's what The Hole Thing is. It's a killer caterpillar."

Sir Ollie double-gulped and looked at Sir Seth. "Wow. Sounds double-gulp scary to me."

Sir Seth just laughed and poked him on the shoulder. "So it's a good thing you're a Mighty Knight, right?"

"Yeah. Right," Sir Ollie had to agree. "But uh...what does a killer 'pillar look like?"

"Well, a killer 'pillar looks a little bit like a lot of things," Betty started to explain. "But mostly, it's a hee-yoo-normous big blue caterpillar about the size of six buses. And that's bad enough. But it also has these long heat-seeking feelers that it sends creeping around out in front of it and when a 'pillar feeler finds you...WHAP! It coils around your legs and runs up your body and into your ears. Then, ever so slowly, it drains the brains right out of your head—and has them for dinner!" Betty paused to take a breath. "At least, that's what I've heard."

"D-d-drains your brains?" Sir Seth stuttered.

"For dinner?" Sir Ollie gasped.

"You're both right!" Betty growled. "So now do you understand what a Thing is? It's a killer caterpillar...that drains your brains...and lives in a cave...at the top of the mountain!"

"And just how does this, um, 'big blue caterpillar' create the feeders, I wonder?" Elynor smirked, each word wrapped in icy disdain.

"You're the queen—you should know!" Betty snapped back equally as icily. She paused to let that sink in. "But since someone has FINALLY asked me what's happening up here, I'll be happy to explain. The Hole Thing hates the cold. So..."

But before either of them could say anything more, a deep, rumbling grumbling ended her sentence.

Sir Seth grabbed the cuff of Elynor's coat. "What's that?"

"It's a feeder!" she said, trying to stay calm, but her large almond eyes were almost the same size as Sir Seth's shield. "Hurry, we must find somewhere to hide."

Sir Seth quickly looked around at all the acres of

empty snow. "Hide? Where can we hide on the side of a mountain?"

Betty the Yeti pointed up to the top of the mountain. "Well, you can go up there and hole up with The Hole Thing—I'm sure he'd love to keep you warm!" she grinned a large evil grin. "Or you can stay here with your queen and get buried under ten billion tons of snow!" Then she threw back her head and cackled her hideous stringy-thinged laugh. "I'm going back to my cave."

And with that, the huge yucky yeti got back on her super-fast icicle sled and schussed back up the mountain…leaving the elf, the two chivalrous knights and, of course, their gallant horse Shasta, to escape the treacherous wall of snow barreling down the north face of the mountain!

"Another fine mess you've gotten us into, Sir Ollie!" Sir Seth sighed. "Now what are we going to do?"

"Quick! We can hide by those rocks until the snow has passed," Elynor said, pointing to a small rocky crag. "It's our only chance!"

At first, they made their way toward the rocks quite easily—almost everywhere, the top of the snow was crisply packed, so they could walk quickly without falling through. In other places, they could even sit and slide like rollicking, frolicking otters down the icy snow.

"Whooeeeee!" Sir Ollie hooted at the top of his voice. "This is almost as much fun as sliding down the bannister at Poxley Castle!"

It was right about then that all the fun began to go wrong.

They hadn't gone far when Sir Seth and Elynor and Shasta ran smack into the waiting, wide-open arms of a sprawling snagglefoot bush. Which stopped them dead in their tracks...while Sir Ollie simply kept on sliding.

And in that instant, Sir Seth knew that by the time they could work themselves free, they wouldn't be able to catch up to Sir Ollie, no matter how hard they tried. The now out-of-control Sir Ollie would be long, loooong gone...

"Heeeey, Ollieeeeeeeeeee, don't worry about us!" Sir Seth shouted to him at the top of his voice. "We'll head up the mountain to stop Betty! You go down the mountain and warn the people of Nhu Kaachuuuuuuu...!"

But before Sir Ollie could warn anybody about anything, he ran into a few problems of his own.

First, he hit a huge lumpy hump in the hard-packed snow and found himself suddenly hurtling downhill backwards—faster and faster, then faster than that—looking over one shoulder, desperately trying to find something to grab. But everywhere he looked, all he saw was the busily passing blur of slippery slopes and white, icy snow.

At this point, Sir Ollie realized it was a good thing that he was a Mighty Knight of Right & Honor, otherwise it could have been very, very easy to be very, very scared.

"I've...got to get...turned around," he told himself. "I've gotta...dig in my heels or grab something...I've got to get stopped."

Just then he hit another huge, hard hump of snow. The next thing Sir Ollie knew, he was cartwheeling head over heels—backwards—completely out of control. In fact, he was somersaulting so ferociously fast, he quickly became whirlingly, twirlingly disoriented and dazed and dreamily dizzy, and not at all sure which way was up. Or down. Or where he was going.

Then he stopped dead in his tracks! Dazed and amazed and gasping for air.

For a long time, Sir Ollie sat there silently stunned, watching his white huffs of breath filling the frosty air between his knees.

Slowly, he looked around at the claw-shaped snagglefoot bush that had snagged him and stopped him in the teeniest, tiniest nick of time. He had come to a sudden skidding stop at the edge of a steep, rocky ledge. Which sat at the dizzying top of a knee-knocking two-mile-and-forty-one-foot-high drop. All the long, long, long way down at the bottom was the itsy-bitsy little village of Nhu Kaachu.

Sir Ollie's hammering heart was pounding so loudly he was sure they could hear it all the way down there in Nhu Kaachu. He became aware that there was someone else with him.

"Are...you...quite all right, sir knight?" a soft bell-like

voice asked from nearby but far away at the same time.

"Y-y-yes. I think I'm okay," Sir Ollie stammered in a blurry haze, struggling to get the world undizzified and back to normal. He could feel himself slowly becoming Sir Ollie all over again. "Give me a minute. Am I still... upside down?"

"You were very, very lucky," the soft voice assured him.

"Who are you...?" Sir Ollie started to say. But when he looked around, there was no one anywhere to be seen.

4 A Nasty, Nail-Gnawing Decision

Sir Seth reached out and snagged Shasta just as a mountainous mass of rumbling, tumbling snow thundered past them with a MEGANORMOUS, ear-numbing roar— missing them by mere inches.

"Ohhhhh boy, that was too close for comfort!" Sir Seth gasped, still clinging to Shasta, who was still clinging to him. "This old snagglefoot bush sure saved our lives," he sighed, as he began pulling at the clinging claw-shaped vines wrapped around his feet.

Elynor watched as the massive feeder slid down onto The Flats and slowed to a stop. "We were very fortunate indeed," she agreed, "but I'm afraid we've come too far west now. Which means we'll have to go up Kill Hill to get to the top of the mountain."

"Kill Hill?" Sir Seth looked with surprise into her dark almond eyes. "You mean there's a hill worse than the one we just came down?"

Elynor shuddered at the thought. "Oh, much worse! Kill Hill is so steep it's almost straight-up-and-down steep...but it's by far the fastest way to get to Betty's cave."

Sir Seth thought about it for a moment, then looked up at Elynor. "Betty's cave? We don't want to go to Betty's cave. It's The Hole Thing that's causing the avalanches, not Betty!"

Elynor angrily put her hands on her hips and leaned closer. "Sir Seth, when are you going to realize there isn't a great big blue bug somewhere up there in a hole. Betty is causing all of the avalanches!" Elynor sighed. "And she very nearly killed you just now!"

"Yeah? So how do you know it was Betty?" He shrugged.

Elynor sighed again. "Because Kaachuian legends are full of how evil Betty the Yeti is. But there's not one word anywhere about a big blue caterpillar."

Sir Seth looked her straight in the eye. "Yeah? Well, y'know what? I'll betcha there is a big blue killer 'pillar up there! And y'know something else, your majesty? I double betcha when we get up there, Betty the Yeti will even help us find him."

Elynor looked down at Sir Seth with worry darkening her eyes. "Betty the Yeti? Help us? Never!"

Sir Seth drew his sword and stood up. "Well, there's only one way to find out. Let's ride!"

Elynor looked down in thought for a long while. Then she looked at Sir Seth. "Yes, I agree. But! Before we go, I must ask you one question," she said in her fascinating little-girl voice.

At once, Sir Seth knew this was going to be serious. "Okay. What's the question?"

She paused, trying to think of the right words. "I know what you are going to say, but try to understand...we don't have time to do everything."

Sir Seth looked into her eyes. "That's not a question."

"Then let me put it this way: you do understand that we cannot go looking for Sir Ollie right now," she said, then paused again, letting the thought find its way into his mind. "There isn't enough time to search for him and to go back up to Betty's cave before the avalanche comes. We can only look for Sir Ollie when our quest has ended."

Sir Seth shivered at the thought. "But by then, it might be too late...," he started to say.

"Perhaps yes," she agreed. "Perhaps not. The time has come for you to decide what is the right and knightly thing to do. Should you look for your friend? Or should you help me stop the avalanches? There isn't time to do both."

A hundred thousand thoughts tumbled hurriedly, worriedly, through Sir Seth's rushing mind, like clothes tumbling over each other in a dryer. As a Mighty Knight of Right & Honor, he simply could not leave his best friend stranded somewhere out there, alone in the snow. It just wasn't the Mighty Knightly thing to do. But! Deep down in his heart, he also realized that Elynor was right... it would take too much time to find Sir Ollie right now. And if the avalanche came before he and Elynor could find him, then he and Sir Ollie and Elynor and all the people of Nhu Kaachu would be buried, too. Besides, Sir Ollie might already have found his own way down the mountain and was waiting for them, all safe and sound. Maybe he had already warned the people of Nhu Kaachu!

Or maybe he was still down there somewhere...

How could Sir Seth leave Sir Ollie? It just wasn't a part of the Mighty Knights' code of honor.

For the first time in his life, Sir Seth's mind just wouldn't let him make a decision.

Then, from nowhere, a sudden thought arrived.

"I've got it!" Sir Seth brightened and turned to Elynor. "Why don't you look for Betty's cave? And I'll stay here and look for Sir Ollie."

Elynor put her hand on his. "Sir Seth, without someone to guide you, you'll never find Sir Ollie in these endless mountains. You could look up here for years and years and never find him." She put a hand on his shoulder. "Besides, if I'm ever to convince Betty to help us, I'll need a knight as honorable as you by my side."

Sir Seth thought about it for about two more seconds.

He deep-deep-down hated to leave Sir Ollie, but he knew Elynor was right...they just had to leave Sir Ollie on his own. For now, anyhow.

It was a terrible decision to make.

But it was the right thing to do.

And Sir Seth just hoped that next time they met, Sir Ollie would punch him on the shoulder and grin and forgive him. And they would still be friends, just like always.

Sarinda Whind

Sir Ollie had never felt so alone in his entire life as he did right there and right then, without his best friend, Sir Seth, standing beside him.

All he could see everywhere he looked was miles and miles of nothing but more and more miles and miles of empty, windblown, white snow...except here and there, where the massive rocky outcrops had stuck their noses out for a look. And far, far below, he could see the uppermost tips of the tops of the snow-covered evergreen trees. And that's all there was to see for about two million miles in every direction—which was as far as Sir Ollie could see.

"I sure hope Seth's all right," he said to himself. "I miss him already."

He slowly began unwinding the long tangles of tendrils of the snagglefoot bush that had snagged him and tangled him up from his head to each toe. And by doing it, had quite likely saved his life.

Sir Ollie took another long look all around. For the first time he could remember, he found himself all on his own. With nothing but blowing snowy nothingness in every direction. Or so he thought.

"You know, dear, you're a very lucky young man," a kindly voice whispered into his ear. "You must realize by now that you shouldn't have come up here all by yourself."

"Huh?" Sir Ollie said, looking all around. "Who are you?"

"Oh, how very forgetful of me," the voice whispered again. "I am Sarinda Whind."

"Pleased to meet you, Sarinda," Sir Ollie said, turning completely around in a circle. "But, uh, where are you?"

"Oh, I'm all around you," the kindly voice whispered into his ear. "I can see you, but you can't see me because 'Sarinda Whind' is the Kaachuian way of saying 'the south wind.'"

"You're the wind?" Sir Ollie said excitedly, still pulling the tangle of vines from his legs. "I didn't know the wind was...a person."

"Oh yes, I'm a person exactly like you, except I don't have a body."

Then, right there in midair, just a few feet in front of his nose, Sir Ollie could vaguely make out the lined, see-through face of a smiling, kindly old lady who, for a fleeting moment, looked just like his grandmother.

"I always come up here on nice days such as this.

You see, I'm much too old to be a blustery blizzard or gustering gale any more. So now I'm just a bit of a breeze, which I must admit, I much, much prefer. Uttar Hawa is the mighty north winter wind you find here most of the time. But enough about me. What brings you all the way up here to Ah Ah Kaachu?"

Sir Ollie avoided her question. "If you're the wind, why can't you blow down—or go down—to Nhu Kaachu and tell the people there really is an avalanche coming?!"

"An avalanche? Oh dear, dear me, not another one!"

"Oh, this one's not just another one," Sir Ollie said, spreading his arms wide. "This one's gonna be... HUNORMOUS! That's why we've gotta get down there and warn them."

"Ohhhhh, I would if I could but I can't," Sarinda Whind whispered softly. "Unfortunately, the people of Nhu Kaachu have grown so used to the sound of my voice, they simply don't hear what I say anymore. Only someone like you, who's new to Nhu Kaachu, can hear me down there."

Sir Ollie pulled the last snaggle free from his knees. "Well then, can you help me get to Nhu Kaachu?"

"Yes, yes, of course. The fastest way, by far, is through The Mids."

"The Mids?" Sir Ollie echoed. "What are The Mids?"

"They're the Snow Fleas' secret tunnels inside the mountain," she whispered into his ear. "They run from the bottom all the way up to the top."

"Sounds kinda scary to me."

"Oh, indeed they can be very scary. But I hear it's the fastest way to get to Nhu Kaachu." She paused, then added, "If you don't run into Ghu, of course."

Sir Ollie stopped in his tracks. "Goo? What kind of goo?"

"Oh, don't worry about Ghu, dear," Sarinda said with a sigh. "I'm sure the whole thing is just another one of those silly old folk tales."

But Sir Ollie suddenly wanted to hear more. "A folk tale about what?"

"Oh, about a monster called Ghu who is supposed to live in The Mids."

"Monster! What kind of monster?"

Sarinda paused, thinking. "Well, um, I've never actually seen Ghu myself, but the stories all say Ghu is just a great big glob of green goo." She paused, then brightened. "But even if all the stories are true, how scary can a glob of green goo be?"

Sir Ollie stood up on jellyfish knees. "I sure hope you're right. Well, c'mon, let's go. How do I get in there?"

"There's an entrance just over there, dear." Sarinda pointed the way, then began breezing along just in front of Sir Ollie, looking over her shoulder.

Sir Ollie drew his sword. "Okay. But how will I be able to see when I get inside?"

"All of the passageways are lit by a strange glowing

light," Sarinda explained as they reached the steaming opening to The Mids. "It's sort of a gloomy, eerie orange glow. But where it comes from, I really don't know."

Sir Ollie stopped dead in his tracks. "Whoa, whoa, whoa. I want to make sure I've got this right. You want ME to go into some SPOOKY old tunnel—with maybe a MONSTER?"

Sarinda Whind had never thought of it quite that way. "Well, I must admit, it does sound rather ooky and spooky. But... it is the fastest way to Nhu Kaachu. Besides, the lava doesn't come up through the mountain. Just the heat does. So you'll be fine."

Sir Ollie would have stopped dead in his tracks all over again, but he still hadn't started after stopping the last time. "Lava? What lava?"

"Oh! Silly me." Sarinda giggled with embarrassment. "I forgot to mention there's an old volcano under the mountain—but only the heat from the lava comes up through The Mids."

"Green gooey monsters. Ooky dark tunnels. Heated by lava." Sir Ollie sighed. "Y'know, if someone wrote a book about me, no one would believe it."

"You'll be absolutely fine, dear. Now, off you go...," Sarinda urged him gently.

Sir Ollie slowly made his way up to the opening and looked inside. And at once, Sir Ollie—the way Sir Ollie always does—began to get nervous.

"You're right, it sure looks pretty ooky and spooky in there..."

And that's about all he was able to say before he tripped over the edge of the ledge at the lip of the cave. And fell in.

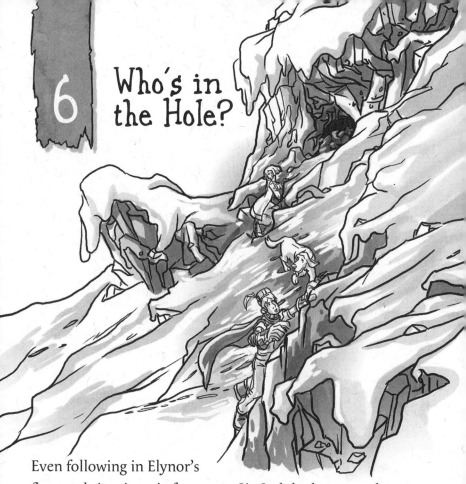

6 Who's in the Hole?

Even following in Elynor's
flattened size-sixty-six footsteps, Sir Seth had to struggle
to make his way through the knee-deep blowing snow.
Elynor glanced over her shoulder and knelt down on one
knee, waiting for Sir Seth and Shasta to catch up.

"Well, we're almost there," she said, looking up at the
narrow mouth of the cave in the side of the mountain.

"Good," Sir Seth sighed, huffing and puffing in the
thin air. "But how do we know whose cave this is?"

"We don't know," Elynor had to admit.

Without another word and like the true Mighty Knight

that he was, Sir Seth rose to his feet. "Well, c'mon, there's only one way to find out..."

Wearily, the three valiant venturers clambered with semi-revived vim and half-hearted vigor through the knee-deep snow until they stood in front of the ominous, dark opening.

Sir Seth peered up at the massive overhanging ledge of deep snow that had piled up above the slitty entrance to the cave. "Well, it's a cave. That's for sure."

"A cave, yes, but whose cave?" Elynor said in her soft way.

"Let's get inside and have a look, before that huge overhang decides to let go and bury us all."

Gripping the raggedy edge of the huge overhanging ledge with both hands, Sir Seth slowly pulled himself up to the opening and cautiously peered in through the narrow rocky slit that formed the mouth of the cave. As his eyes grew accustomed to the dark, he discovered there was absolutely nothing to see inside—except for a bunch of big boulders and lots and lots of nothing at all, all bathed in a faint eerie orange light, and the steady, summery flow of warm air coming from somewhere deep down.

"Can you see anything?" Elynor called up to him.

"Nope, nothing. Just lots and lots of big rocks. The whole place smells like Sir Ollie's socks, but at least it's nice and warm in here."

Sir Seth put one arm around Shasta, holding her back. He cautiously stuck his head farther into the ominous

opening to help his eyes adjust to the eerie dim light.
But there still wasn't much more to see. Everywhere
he looked, there were simply piles and piles of rocks.
And a long, long, jaggedy tunnel that disappeared down
into the shadowy gloom.

"Y'know, I think somebody might live here," he
said over one shoulder.

"Oh?" Elynor called back up. "What makes you
think so?"

"Well, there's a bunch of really, really HEEEE-YUGE
boulders piled up in front of the entrance," he said as
he wriggled his shoulders inside the small opening.
"But that's about all I can see."

"Boulders?" Elynor wondered out loud.

"Yep. Lots of them. And they didn't get here by
themselves," he quickly pointed out. "Somebody went
to a lot of work to put them here. Because, for sure,
this slitty little entrance used to be a lot bigger."

Then Sir Seth remembered something Betty had said.
"Hey, remember Betty said The Hole Thing hates the
cold? Well, it's pretty warm in here. I think this might
be The Hole Thing's hole."

"Hole Thing?" Elynor snapped, nervously looking
around. "You're n-not *still* going on about this whole
Hole Thing thing, are you?"

"Well, it's either Betty's cave or The Thing's hole. So
let's find out. Um, yoo hooooo," Sir Seth whispered,
trying not to upset whatever might be lurking inside,

in case it was napping. "Anybody home?"

His voice echoed hollowly off the raggedy, jaggedy rock walls, then faded away. Shasta came huffing and puffing excitedly up beside him and gave him a great big wet lick. He patted his faithful steed on her head and turned back to Elynor. "Y'know, maybe I was wrong. It sure is quiet in there. Maybe it's just an empty old cave after all."

Elynor didn't know what to say. "I'm sorry, Sir Seth, I really don't know. There are places where even I dare not go—and until right now, this was definitely one of them."

Sir Seth stared back into the shadowy gloom, then leaned forward and called a little bit louder. "Uh, Mister Thing! It's Sir Seth Thistlethwaite and Lady Elynor, the Faerie Queen of Ah Ah Kaachu. We were, y'know, sorta wondering if we could talk to you for a minute."

But the only sound he could hear was the endless echo of his own voice disappearing hollowly down the long, empty tunnel.

"There doesn't seem to be anyone here," he said, poking his head back outside.

"Now what are we going to...," Elynor started to say, but before she could finish, a rumbling, grumbling outside finished her sentence for her.

"Oh no! ANOTHER feeder's coming!" she shouted shrilly, looking up. "And it's almost on top of us!"

She tried and tried to clamber up beside Sir Seth but her size-sixty-six snowshoe-elf feet kept slipping and sliding and getting caught in the jumble of rocks at the mouth of the cave.

Sir Seth reached down for her hand. "Quick, my lady! Grab my hand!"

With a Mighty Knightly heave, he managed to pull Elynor up beside him, and they both scrambled in through the ominous opening. Shasta scurried in close behind just as another huge snowslide rumbled past the cave, taking rocks from the opening with it as it thundered down toward The Flats.

The two of them stood in open-mouthed awe, wordlessly watching the tons and tons and tons of thundering boulders and snow smashing and bashing their way past the mouth of the cave.

With her eyes the size of two saucers, Elynor anxiously looked down at Sir Seth. "Oh, when you see one this close, an avalanche is ten thousand times worse than I imagined. We absolutely can't let this happen to Nhu Kaachu!"

"Well, if this is The Hole Thing's hole, we're in the right place to start stopping it."

Elynor slowly scanned the eerie echoing gloom all around them. "I sincerely hope you're right. But this place looks rather empty to me."

Then Sir Seth knelt down on one knightly knee. "Maybe not. Come here, look at this."

Elynor knelt down beside him. "What is it?"

"Look at these long gouges. It looks like someone's

been pushing all these huge rocks across the floor and piling them up here, trying to block this entrance."

Elynor ran her hand across one of the deep gashes. "I wonder why?" she wondered out loud, then looked anxiously down at Sir Seth.

He looked back up to the opening they had just come through. "Y'know, I've got a creepy feeling that something VERY, VERY BIG has been pushing all these huuuuunormous rocks up against the entrance."

Elynor didn't have to say a word. The worry in her eyes said it all.

So Sir Seth said it for her. "I think maybe Betty was telling the truth. I bet this is The Hole Thing's hole."

Elynor double-gulped. Although she still didn't wholly believe that The Hole Thing was really a real thing, it had definitely become a very real possibility.

She stood up and looked at Sir Seth. "What are we going to do, sir knight? We can't go outside, in case the avalanche comes. And we can't stay here, in case something else comes."

Sir Seth put his hand on his sword. "Fear not, my lady! My mighty broadsword will fend off any foes, no matter how fearsome or foul."

Suddenly, Shasta started snarling and snapping at something she saw on the floor.

"Sir Seth! Look over there!" Elynor gasped in horror. "What's that?"

They both stared at a very, very scary and very, very

unhairy, long blue lizard-like feeler slowly oozing toward them across the stone floor.

"Caw! Caw! Caw! Caw!" Sir Seth instantly sprang into action, automatically crowing the Mighty Knights' secret warning. "It's one of The Hole Thing's brain-feeding feelers! Quickly, my lady, to arms! Here, take my lance..."

And with that, the time for words had passed them both by—Sir Seth's Mighty Knightly instincts took over. Without thought for his own self or safety, he gallantly stepped forth in front of the fair Elynor, and gripping his sturdy sword tightly with both hands, he swung it in a towering, overpowering overhead arc and brought it down hard—with a thundering, feeler-whacking THWACK!—on the slinky snake-like thing creeping across the cave floor.

At first, there was a tense, pulse-pounding pause. Followed by a lot of not much at all. Then, in a lightning-like flash, the flattened blue feeler whirled and flew back down the long stone floor of the tunnel—and disappeared out of sight, with Shasta frantically chasing after it, howling and growling at the top of her voice.

"Shasta...no, no!" Sir Seth called after her. "Come back here."

"Is it gone?" Elynor whispered between her ten frightened fingers in front of her face.

"Yes, my lady. Once again, my sturdy sword has saved the day."

But just when Elynor thought they were safe, a second insidiously sinewy thing began slithering silently toward them from the other side of the tunnel. Before she could shriek, speak, or squeak, the long, blue, brain-draining feeler lashed out and seized Sir Seth by the ankles. With a jerk, it tugged itself tight and pulled him right off his feet. Then it slowly started snaking its way up his leg—heading straight for his ears and toward his brain.

However, stirred on and spurred on by Sir Seth's gallant feeler-flattening feat, Elynor quickly reached down, and grasping one of her size-sixty-six snowshoes, she pulled it easily from one of her feet. Then, swinging it over her head like a size-sixty-six sword, she brought the heavy snowshoe down with the same feeler-flattening force as Sir Seth's—sending the slithering feeler scurrying in a blazing blue blur back down the tunnel and out of sight.

Sir Seth stared at her in speechless surprise. "Wow, I thought those snowshoes were part of your feet..."

Elynor couldn't help smiling an embarrassed little smile as she leaned the large, heavy snowshoe back against the wall. "You didn't really believe I had size-sixty-six feet, did you?"

"Uh, yeah," Sir Seth said, still surprised. "I believe pretty much everything you say."

Just then, from somewhere deep down inside the dark echoing black hole, a huuuuunormous deep-throated roar like rolling thunder filled the cave with a rushing, gushing overwhelming tsunami of sound...

"YUMMY, YUMMY, HERE I COME TO DRAIN YOUR BRAINS AND FILL MY TUMMY!"

Elynor was squeezing Sir Seth's hand so hard he was sure every bone in each finger was broken.

"It's...The Hole Thing!" she managed to mutter, finally believing it was real. "And it knows we're here!"

With his trusty sword clutched tightly in his other hand, Sir Seth peered into the eerie gray gloom, warily waiting for The Hole Thing to appear. "It's The Thing, all right. I've never seen Shasta this snarly and snappy and so full of fight."

Elynor looked down at Shasta. Every golden hair on Shasta's back was standing straight up on end—and each time she let out a frantic "Woo! Woo! Woo!", her front legs jumped right off the ground, the way most horses' do when they're just a bit jittery.

Then...slowly but surely, down the dark tunnel to their right, another unhairy and very, very scary blue killer 'pillar tentacle began feeling its way toward them out of the gloom.

"Look out, my lady!" Sir Seth cried, stepping up beside Elynor. "Here comes another one of those brain-draining feelers."

"Oh, sir knight, what are we going to do?"

"Do?" Sir Seth said, working his hand free. "There's only one thing we can do—we'll just have to stand here and fight! Because a Mighty Knight never backs down when there's a wrong to make right. No matter what fearsome foe he must face."

But neither of them was ready for the fearsome foe they were about to meet face-to-face. The instant she saw The Hole Thing for the first time, Elynor was so suddenly shaken with shock, she tried six times to shout but each time, nothing came out.

"What is it, my lady?"

Sir Seth stared squinty-eyed down the long dark tunnel, wondering what Elynor was seeing. Then, with a heart-stopping start, a cold chill suddenly ran up both arms and into his heart. He realized he wasn't staring down a long, dark tunnel at all. Instead, he was staring down into the killer caterpillar's mountainous, wide-open...

MOUTH!

"Oh no!" was all Sir Seth could think of to say. "We're not looking into a cave, we're looking at the inside of The Hole Thing's mouth!"

The Hole Thing's gaping mouth was the same size and color as the dark rock walls of the cave all around it. Which made it look as if it were part of the cave. Sir Seth was so hypnotized by the huge, open mouth, he forgot all about the hairless blue brain-draining feeler silently sliding along the side of the wall. Then, without any warning, the lizard-like thing lashed out from the shadowy shelter of the rocks and wound itself around and around and around Sir Seth's legs in its tightening, frightening snake-like grip. Then it slowly began winding its way up his legs, heading straight for his ears.

"Shasta! Elynor! Help!" Sir Seth frantically shouted.

But before the fearsome, freezing feeler could creep an inch farther, a golden ball of flying fur flew past Sir Seth in a snapping, snarling teeth-gnashing flash and chomped down hard on The Hole Thing's vile 'pillar feeler.

There was a slight surprised pause, followed by a spine-chilling howl of pain.

Then everything quickly went quiet all over again.

"Sir Seth, are you all right?" Elynor asked in her calm, quiet way.

"Yes, my lady. But The Thing's feelers are not only scary and strong, they're freezing cold, too," Sir Seth said with surprise. "It wouldn't take long for one of them to freeze you, too, through and through and through."

Still lying flat on his back and frantically pumping his legs, Sir Seth desperately pushed himself across the floor to where Elynor was waiting. He was about to grab her hand and make a run for the entrance when, without warning, another violent tremor shook the whole Hole, sending a thick sea of snow thundering down the mountainside to the mouth of the cave. As it did, the entire Hole went as black as licorice inside, without so much as a glimmer of the strange orange glow that had been lighting the inside of the tunnel.

Then, bit by bit by bit, bright daylight came creeping in as the thundering snowslide outside began pulling the huge boulders, one by one, away from the mouth of The Hole. And down at the other end of the cave, in the growing bright daylight, the same angry, ear-shattering roar cried out...

YUMMY,
YUMMY,
HERE I COME
TO DRAIN
YOUR BRAINS
AND FILL MY TUMMY!

Sir Seth knew he must reach down deep inside and find the determination to stand up and fight like the valiant Mighty Knight that he was. He got to his feet, and holding his sword straight out before him, stared down the slowly brightening tunnel, straight into the caterpillar's ghastly, gaping mouth filled with long, hanging strings of gooey saliva and things.

Then, before anyone had time to react, three freezing feelers suddenly lashed out at the same time and in a lightning-fast flash, they wrapped themselves around and around and around Sir Seth. And Shasta! And Elynor, too!

Then, bit by bit, The Hole Thing slowly began drawing all three of them toward its anxiously waiting, wide open mouth.

Sir Seth looked over at Shasta. "Y'know, it's at times like this that I sure wish Sir Ollie was here..."

In the Midst of the Mids

After tripping and falling face-first into the murk at the mouth of The Mids, Sir Ollie tumbled head over heels, floating slowly, almost dreamily, for what seemed like a long, long time before finally, mouth wide open, with an enormous, echoing KUH-PLOSHHHHH, he fell flat on his back, in a huge pond of...steaming hot water!

"Huh? Hot water?" he thought to himself, as he frantically kicked his way back up to the surface. "What's a lake doing in the middle of a mountain? And...how am I ever gonna get dry?"

With his last gasp of breath, Sir Ollie popped up into the eerily echoing orange glow that shimmered and glimmered up and down the gray rocky roof of the much-talked-about Mids. He took a quick look around at his strange dark surroundings as he struggled to keep his head above water. His soggy winter clothes and heavy Mighty Knights boots tried to drag him back under. But, fortunately for him, he had landed near the edge of the pond, where it was just a short swim to shore.

With a mighty knightly heave, Sir Ollie pulled himself out, then slumped down onto one arm, completely out of breath and a little bit dizzy, watching the drops of water drip from his face to the floor.

"Hey, howyuh doin', brother?" a teeny weeny voice

greeted him from somewhere nearby.

Sir Ollie looked around but couldn't see anyone. "I'm wet and I'm freezin'," he grumped to no one at all.

"Well, duhhhhh!" the tiny voice said with what sounded like a smile. "Like, who goes swimmin' in the middle of winter!"

"I didn't 'go swimming.' I fell in here," Sir Ollie grumpily grunted again, looking around to see who was talking. "Who are you, anyhow...and where are you? I can hardly hear you."

"Try lookin' down here on yer foot," the little voice shouted up to him. Which is hard for someone as small as a flea to do—because Sir Ollie was almost too tall to hear what a flea says at all. Can you imagine how loud a flea has to squeak for his flea-speak to be heard all the way up where your ears are? That's why you've never heard a flea chit. Or chat. Or holler. Or shout. Or make any sort of sound that sounds as though it had made any sound at all. Because the more you think about it, the more you'll agree...any shout that comes out of a flea will be about as loud as the bark of a tree. Which is a shout about as loud as no shout at all.

"Mind if I jump up on yer nose?"

"Sure. C'mon up," Ollie said, still looking around, happy to have someone for company...even if he couldn't see who it was.

Suddenly, right there, on the end of his nose, appeared the smiling wee face of a little white flea.

"So can you see me now, brother?" he said in his itsy-bitsy voice, moving closer.

"Yeah...sorta," Sir Ollie said, trying to focus on the end of his nose. Have you ever tried to look at a little white dot on the end of your nose? Go ahead, do it right now. There, see what I mean? It's not as easy as you think. First of all, you go cross-eyed. Then the end of your nose goes double.

"Hey, brother. I'm Flit, the wallah of the Snow Fleas," he smiled happily. "I can't tell yuh how truly super-exciting it is t'meet yuh! Last time we had a visitor in here was way back in the winter of '33, when I was just knee-high to a gnat. So uh, tell me, what brings you all the way up here to The Mids? It could only be one of three things...you're a tourist, you're lost, or you're crazy." He paused. "Or maybe all three."

Sir Ollie avoided the question. "Hi, Flit. Uh, what's a wallah?"

"Well, I'm sorta the mayor of the mountain, y'might say, and your tour guide while you're here. And as such, it's my official duty to welcome you to the wunnerful,

wunnerful world of The Mids."

But before Sir Ollie could answer, the entire cave shuddered and shook all over. Then went still. Then it shuddered and shook all over again, spraying a shower of small stones and pebbles in every direction. Again. And again. And again.

Then once more after that.

Before it finally went still.

"Uh ohhhhh...," Sir Ollie started to say nervously.

"Hey, no sweat, brother," Flit smiled happily. "It's just another one of yer avalanches fillin' up The Flats with snow. Happens all the time. But you'll be safe inside The Mids with me. So, uh, what brings you here?"

Sir Ollie bowed, with Flit still on the end of his nose. "I'm Sir Ollie Everghettz of the Mighty Knights of Right & Honor."

"You're who? Of the what?"

"Never mind. I'll tell you later!" Sir Ollie said anxiously. "Right now, I have to get down to Nhu Kaachu, like lickety split. Will you help me do that?"

Flit scratched his head, seeming suddenly sort of upset. "Nhu Kaachu? Really? Why do you wanna go there?"

"To warn them of the avalanche."

"Ah, don't worry about them. They wouldn't worry about you."

Sir Ollie didn't have time to get into a long discussion. "The Mighty Knights are sworn to help everyone, everywhere, no matter what. And this won't just be any old avalanche. It'll be the GOLD MEDAL GRANDPAPPY of 'em all—the worst one Ah Ah Kaachu has ever seen! So please help me get down to Nhu Kaachu."

Flit found his carefree smile again. "Yeah, sure thing, brother...but 'the worst one ever'? Lemme have a look t'see if this pile of snow is as big as you say. Don't go away."

Then, in a blink, and as quick as a wink, Flit flew off in a flash.

"Did he say 'Don't go away'?" Sir Ollie laughed to himself. "Where did he think I was going to go—sopping wet from my nose down to my toes, in the middle of winter?"

But before he could move, Sir Ollie felt the presence of Sarinda Whind once again.

"Oh goodness gracious me. Just look at you, Sir Ollie," she sighed with motherly concern. "Get out of those wet clothes this minute before you catch bubonic pneumonia. You can spread them out on that ledge over there," she whispered. "I'll blow-dry them for you in a jiffy."

Sir Ollie pulled off one of his silver Mighty Knights rubber boots and poured out about a gallon of water, three minnows, two frogs, and a crayfish the size of his hand.

"It's a good thing it's this nice and warm in here. How come it's so summery inside the mountain and so wintery out there?"

"Well, as I said, you can thank that lava for that, dear.

Luckily for you, it keeps everything roasty and toasty inside the mountain. Including the water."

Ollie sat back down and looked around at his dreary, eerie surroundings and wondered what Sir Seth would do if he were here.

"Gee, y'know, I can't stop wondering about Sir Seth," he said to no one at all, suddenly feeling guilty that he was inside where it was safe, while his friends were all out there somewhere in the snow. "I sure hope they're okay. Same with Elynor. And Shasta, too! Sarinda, is there some way you could sorta go out and look around and...see if you can find them?"

"Yes, all right. I promise you I'll have a look for them," she assured him softly. "Just as soon as I finish blow-drying your clothes."

Immediately, Sir Ollie felt a bit better. And although it seemed strange to be somewhere without Sir Seth, he knew he'd just have to pull up his socks—when they were dry— and do what any Mighty Knight, anywhere, would do. He, Sir Ollie Everghettz, would go forth and do the right thing and uphold the good name of the Mighty Knights of Right & Honor. He would save the village of Nhu Kaachu, no matter what. Even if he was kinda nervous...and had to do it by himself. All alone. On his own.

Then, from out of nowhere, Flit jumped back up onto his nose.

"C'mon, brother. Hurry up and get dressed," he whooped excitedly in his teeny-weeny voice. "Yer story checks out—that stack of snow stalled out there on The Flats is the biggest I've ever seen. C'mon, we gotta get going. And get going fast!"

"Okay, little brother, I'm ready to ride," Sir Ollie said, excitedly slipping on his pants.

Duty was clearly calling! The feeling felt good in his veins as it surged through his heart. He forgot to be nervous now that there was a job to be done—and people out there who needed his help! He got dressed as fast as he could, amazed that his socks and all of his clothes were already dry and ready to wear.

"Oh, thank you, thank you, Sarinda. I didn't know how I was going to get dry."

Sarinda blew him a kiss that landed lightly on one cheek. "I'm glad I could help. Now off you go."

And then off she flew.

Sir Ollie turned back to his new flea friend. He held high the red and white Mighty Knights garbage-can lid that his dad had helped him paint. "The Mighty Knights of Right & Honor are on their way! What are the Mids like, Flit? How are we gonna get down them?"

"Y'just follow the end of yer nose, brother. I'll be right here to show you the way." Flit smiled over one shoulder. "The Mids are really just a lot of long tunnels that zig and zag all the way down to the bottom of the mountain. But, hey, don't worry! If we have any problems, there are a billion and three Snow Fleas ready to help us out. Any time we need 'em."

Sir Ollie stopped in his tracks. "A billion and three?

"Well, yeah! Hey, you don't think I live here all by myself, do you?"

Sir Ollie thought about it briefly. "No, I guess not. Okay. Ready, little brother? Let's go." He drew a deep breath as he took his first step out into the gloom.

If you want to know what The Mids look like, just run your tongue across the roof of your mouth. Feel all those wrinkly bumps and humps and lumps? Well, that's exactly what the roof of The Mids looks like. Except it gives off an eerie lava-like glow.

Now look in the mirror and open your mouth as wide as it will go. And that's just what the tunnel looked like as it ran down, down, down into the middle of the mountain and disappeared down, down, down, right out of sight.

Sir Ollie stretched out both arms. The tunnel was about four double-armspreads wide, he guessed, and maybe six double-armspreads high. And up ahead, just like Flit said, it twisted and turned and went right out of sight. It was just like looking down the throat of a whale.

"This place sure is double-darn geeky and eeky," he said. "Are you sure we haven't been swallowed by some knight-eating dragon or something like that?"

Sir Ollie, somewhat nervously at first, began picking his way down the white rocky pathway that led down through the middle of the echoing mountain in the eerie orange lava light. He thought for sure the surface would be slippery and wet, but surprisingly enough, it was dry as a dirt road in the middle of summer, making it easy to walk quickly. Except for the loose gravel all along the edges.

"How long do you think it'll take us to get to the bottom?"

Flit looked back over his shoulder. "Ohhhhh, about two hours. Maybe four. Maybe more."

"Four hours!" Sir Ollie shouted with shock. "We've got to go faster than that. How long will it be before the avalanche comes?"

Flit thought about it quickly. "Hard to say. Maybe a minute. Maybe all day."

8 Elynor Makes a Discovery

Sir Seth struggled to get free from The Hole Thing's freezing feelers, but try as hard as he might, his legs flailing in midair, even a Mighty Knight was no match for its strength.

"Oh, sir knight, I can't move," Elynor cried out nervously. "How are we ever going get free?"

"Well, I'm already working on an exit plan," Sir Seth said. "But it's hard to come up with anything when the only thing I can move is my thumbs."

Even Shasta looked at him with big brown sorrowful eyes, unable to help.

But as it turned out, the mountain itself came to Sir Seth's rescue. As the last avalanche passed by, it cleared most of the rocks from around the cave opening. From the wide open mouth of The Hole, an icy wintry wind suddenly came breezing in. Instantly, this turned the freezing blue Hole Thing thirty-two times bluer than the blue it had been before—sending a juddering shudder running clean through to its bones, if there were any bones in there to judder or shudder at all.

The Hole Thing's snaky feelers went instantly limp, dropping Sir Seth, Shasta, and Elynor with three heavy thumpety-thumpety-thumps down onto the cold, hard stone floor. And before you could say "Thelma's thick socks", all three of The Thing's captives scrambled in rubbery-kneed panic toward the open entrance of The Hole.

Then The Thing let out a mighty ear-splitting roar...

"CLOSE THE DOOR! OR
I'LL BLOCK
THE HOLE
WITH YOUR
BONES!"

Everyone instantly froze in their tracks. Sir Seth numbly looked down at Shasta as Shasta numbly looked up at Elynor. Then, in a hurried, worried blur—spurred on by a touch of knee-numbing terror—all three of them tumbled over each other in a mad, tangled scramble to see who would be the first one to get out of The Hole.

As it turned out, Elynor, with her long elfin legs, was first to reach the opening, but as she did, she suddenly stopped dead in her tracks. "Ahhhhh! Now I'm beginning to understand what this whole Hole Thing's all about," she gasped under her breath.

Meanwhile, still running as fast as their six legs would fly, while anxiously looking over their shoulders, Sir Seth and Shasta ran whappity-whappity whap at full speed smack into her back. Sir Seth quickly perked up, wondering what Elynor was talking about. "Um, understand? What are you beginning to understand?"

Elynor excitedly began to explain. "You were the first one to notice those gouges all over the floor inside the entrance. Well, Sir Seth, I guess I have to admit, they probably were made by The Thing shoving all those big boulders up against The Hole to block it—so he could keep the cold out and keep the heat in. Just like you said."

"Yeah? And then?"

"And then, when the snow builds up outside The Hole," she continued, "the heat inside the cave heats the ground all above it. Which melts the snow underneath..."

Suddenly Sir Seth understood and joined in. "Which makes the snow slippery..."

"And that's what makes the avalanches begin!" Elynor finished his sentence.

Even Shasta was so mad she began to growl.

Elynor tromped back to the opening, and in a most uncharacteristic way, began wagging a finger at The Hole Thing. "You should be ashamed of yourself, you selfish, evil, thoughtless old Thing!" she huffed at the top of her voice, growing more upset with every word. "You've been creating all the avalanches from the very beginning, haven't you!"

"Yeah!" Sir Seth agreed. "Come out here and fight like a...a Thing!"

From somewhere deep inside, the huge blue, hole-filling Hole Thing oozed into the bright sunlight streaming into the cave, while still trying to avoid the blustering, bitter cold coming from outside. Sir Seth stood there, mesmerized, listening to his two busily knocking knees, and gaped. And there it was!

The dreaded Hole Thing!

"So...Betty the Yeti was telling the truth!" Elynor gasped when she saw The Hole Thing for real.

Its cold, emotionless, beady little eyes peered out from either side of a pushed-up pug nose that looked like two bullet holes above its cavernous stringy-thinged mouth. And its long, snaky blue feelers writhed around on the ground out in front like six blue pitbull pythons looking for a juicy brain to drain!

Then the huge blue Thing began slowly slithering back into the warmth of its cave.

"Ahhhhh," Elynor sighed to herself. "I think I'm finally beginning to understand what's been happening up here." She called angrily into the cave. "You've been blocking up The Hole, trying to stay warm! Haven't you?"

But The Thing had nothing to say.

Elynor put her hands on her hips and leaned forward. "You could have killed everyone in Nhu Kaachu—but you didn't care, as long as you were warm! You evil, selfish, evil, thoughtless old Thing!"

Sir Seth reached up and took her by the hand. "Come, my lady, let's sit down and share a handful of snow and try to figure out what we're going to do next—now that we know all this new stuff that we know." He shrugged.

"Yes, let's." Elynor smiled down at him. "I must say, you've almost become a Kaachuian, haven't you?"

Rumbling?
What Rumbling?

After almost an hour of making their way down the craggy crevice in the eerie orange lava-lit glow of The Mids, Sir Ollie and his itsy-bitsy Snow Flea friend, Flit, finally stopped to catch their breath. Sir Ollie leaned up against the wall and looked cross-eyed at Flit.

"There's gotta be...a faster way down," he huffed and puffed, wiping his brow. "We're never gonna make it... to Nhu Kaachu in time...walkin' like this."

Flit shrugged. "Hey, it's the fastest way, brother. Unless you want to ride down to Nhu Kaachu on the next avalanche."

Suddenly, Sir Ollie perked up. "Listen! What's that noise?"

"Noise? What noise?" the little flea shouted above the sound of Sir Ollie's huffing and puffing.

"It sounds sorta like a rumbling noise. Can you hear it?"

Flit cocked his head to one side, listening intently. "Rumbling? What rumbling? The only rumblin' you're gonna hear around here is an avalanche out there."

"It sure doesn't sound like an avalanche to me...," said Sir Ollie, his voice trailing off.

The two of them listened as hard as they could, which isn't easy to do, because listening is one of those things you either do or don't do, with no halfway or middle. But from his perch at the end of Sir Ollie's nose, all Flit was able to hear was Sir Ollie's busy breathing and the occasional plip or plop as the occasional drip or drop of water plopped on the pebbles by the side of the path.

"Nope. I don't hear a thing…," Flit started to say, then stopped. "Whoa! Wait a minute, brother. I do, I do, I do!"

As they listened, the faint, faraway rumbling grew louder and louder. And closer and closer.

"Yeah, you're right, brother," Flit agreed. "Something's coming all right!"

"And coming fast, too! What could it be?" Sir Ollie wondered.

But before Flit could utter one more word, an enormous out-of-control boulder suddenly came thundering down the tunnel and slammed into the wall beside them—sending a shower of loose lava rocks rocketing off the sides of the tunnel in every direction—which in turn created a tumbling rockslide that blocked the tunnel. And it all happened in about four seconds flat.

Then everything went suddenly, shockingly still. Sir Ollie and Flit stood there, too tongue-tied to speak, waiting to see what would happen next.

But nothing happened next. Absolutely nothing at all.

"Uh oh," Flit suddenly said to the surrounding silence.

"'Uh oh'? Those two words usually mean trouble," Sir Ollie nervously replied. "Why did you just say 'Uh oh,' little brother?"

"This was no accident!" Flit snorted. "My guess is Ghu did it. And did it on purpose."

Sir Ollie looked around. "You mean, the great big green glob of goo? That Ghu?"

"Oh, I guess I forgot to tell you," Flit said, beginning to grow angry. "Ghu's the dude who thinks he runs things around here. The Snow Fleas have been fightin' with Ghu for four hundred years, but how can a flea the size of me fight a slobbering glob of glop the size of Ghu—and ever hope to win?"

"Sarinda thought he might just be a folklore story," Sir Ollie said hopefully.

"Nope. He's the real deal, all right—a great big wobbly, blobbery mountain of goo, with a great big slobbery, blobbery mouth that fills the tunnel from top to bottom."

Sir Ollie reached for El Gonzo. "And you think this guy, Ghu, did this on purpose?"

"Yep. He wanted to block the tunnel."

"I thought you said this was the safe way down." Sir Ollie snorted. "Why would Ghu do a dumb thing like that?"

"Oh, he thinks The Mids belong to him, brother," Flit explained. "And he goes kuh-razy when anyone else tries to come in here. Of course, we Snow Fleas can flit past him most of the time, without him even knowing we're there. But you're way too big to be a flitter!" Flit smirked, looking back at Sir Ollie. "Besides, he's probably hungry."

"Hungry?" Sir Ollie tightened his grip on El Gonzo. "Uh, what does he eat?"

"Good question," the little flea said, scratching his head. "There's not much in here except fleas, rocks, and lava. And one Mighty Knight. Take your pick."

"Yeah? Well, I can't wait for this guy, Ghu, to get here. I think we should teach him a few Mighty Knightly manners."

"We can do that later," Flit reminded him. "Right now, we've gotta get you down to Nhu Kaachu."

"Yeah, right!" Sir Ollie looked at the solid wall of rocks

blocking the tunnel behind them. "But how? The tunnel's blocked with ten tons of rocks, little brother. How are we gonna get around all this?"

"Well, we could go back up, and try to find another way down, but..." Then he stopped and looked nervously at Sir Ollie. "Whoa, wait a minute. Do you hear what I hear?"

"I sure hear something," Sir Ollie said, turning to look back up the tunnel. "Sort of an ooey-gooey shlurping sound. And I can smell something, too! What's a dead fish doing in here?"

Flit froze with fear. "That's no dead fish, brother. It's Ghu! He's comin' to get us."

Sir Ollie wiped his hands on his shirt. All his Mighty Knight training rushed through his mind, as he once again tightened his grip on El Gonzo and took a quick look around. But wherever Sir Ollie looked, there was nowhere to go. They were well and truly trapped

like two tree toads up a tree—by a solid wall of rocks blocking the tunnel behind them. And a giant glob of wall-to-wall goo about to attack them from the front.

"Get ready, little brother, it looks like the Mighty Knights are in for a pretty good fight."

"You haven't met Ghu," Flit sighed. "Ghu's too big and gooey to fight. And if you can't hit 'im, you can't hurt 'im. So, he'll just swallow you whole, no matter what you try to do."

Sir Ollie was about to argue the point when—from far down the length of the tunnel—Ghu oozed slowly into sight.

Flit was right.

Ghu was big.

No, Ghu was huge.

In fact, Ghu was huger than huge. And much, much more massive than merely mountainous. Let's just say he was so big, he made enormous look small. In fact, you know what? There isn't a "big" word big enough to tell you how big Ghu really is. His shapeless see-through form filled the tunnel from the top to the bottom like a gigantic green dollop of the wubbly mint jelly Sir Ollie's grandmother puts on his lamb.

Sir Ollie triple-gulped the minute he laid eyes on Ghu. "I see what you mean. How can anyone fight something as globby and gooey as that?"

"You can't. Fighting Ghu is just like trying to punch a bowlful of jelly, brother," Flit sighed. "Ghu is too gooey! There's no way you can win."

Immediately, Sir Ollie tried another approach, his mind racing like mad as the green globby thing oozed closer and closer. "Okay, if we can't fight him, can we talk to him?"

"Not really," Flit said, thinking about it. "Oh, he sorta gurgles and grunts sometimes, but that's about all."

Sir Ollie was growing more and more nervous as Ghu slithered closer and closer. "Uh...what d'you think he's gonna do to us?"

"I don't know that either," Flit said, backing up. "Ghu is so slothishly, snailishly slow, I've never been caught."

The words were no sooner out of Flit's mouth than a large gooey globular hole opened up, right about where Ghu's mouth should have been.

Flit ran between Sir Ollie's eyes. "Well, what are we gonna do now, big brother?"

"There's only one thing we can do, Flit," Sir Ollie said, like the true knight he was, as he readied El Gonzo. "A Mighty Knight must stand up and fight for what he knows, in his heart, is the right thing to do!" And with that, he rushed down the length of the tunnel toward the plodding glob, swung his sword, and...watched as it went cleanly through Ghu with ridiculous ease without hurting him at all!

"You missed!" Flit shouted in stunned surprise. "I don't believe it. You call yourself a Mighty Knight...and you missed him completely!"

But Sir Ollie was just as stunned. "I didn't miss him. I just didn't hit him," he called out as he rushed back down the tunnel to join Flit at the wall. "Trying to subdue Ghu is like trying to grab a handful of water."

"Well, big brother, our backs are up against the wall. We've got nowhere to go. You better think of something fast...or in a few minutes we're gonna be Ghu goulash!"

Sir Ollie's mighty mind raced faster than it had ever raced before in his entire knightly life. "Gee, I sure wish Sir Seth was here right now," Sir Ollie sighed under his breath. "He'd know what to do about Ghu."

10 Yackety's Advice

From the mouth of her cave high atop the mountain, Betty the Yeti stood looking forlornly at the sun shining on the brightly sequined snow piled high above the opening to The Hole Thing's hole.

She looked and she sighed.

"You're back already? Why so grumpy?" a deep, warm voice said from somewhere behind her.

"Oh, I just ran into some people from Nhu Kaachu…," Betty said sadly. Followed by a shrug.

"Let's see if I can guess what the problem is, you grumpy old yeti. I'll bet you finally had the chance to be nice for a change and help people out. But what did you do? You growled and grumped and drove them away. Am I right?"

Betty turned and looked into the big brown eyes of her fantabulest best friend, a huge, shaggy-haired Yubetan yak called…

Well, before we go any further, perhaps we should take a quick look at the FAST YAK FACTS handbook and find out a few fast facts about yaks. To begin with, on page one it clearly states:

Fast Yak Fact 1. Yaks are very, very big.

Fast Yak Fact 2: Yaks are very, very hairy.

Fast Yak Fact 3: Yaks love to yak.

But of all the things a yak loves to do, there's definitely no doubt about it—a yak loves to yak best. Then yak and yak some more.

And yak.

And yak.

And yak.

And yak.

And yak.

Until your ears are sore.

So that's why Betty called her friend..."Yackety."

Because Yackety loved to yak.

And yak. And yak.

"Well, I *did* try to warn them," Betty sighed forlornly. "Just like I tried to warn them ten years ago! But they all turned out to be mean, mad, and miserable, just like everyone else. Well, maybe that little knight wasn't so bad. And his dog was kinda cute. But there was a tall elf called Elynor who was just plain deep-down mean and awful—blaming me for every avalanche that ever happened anywhere in Ah Ah Kaachu! Ever! Everyone thinks that the avalanches are my fault!"

"Now, now, you and I know the avalanches aren't your fault, dear," Yackety said, trying to calm her friend. "You've tried and tried to warn the people, but..."

"Oh, Yackety," Betty sobbed, "why won't they listen?" Then Betty froze in utter spluttering, muttering horror. "Oh no! OH NO! What have I just done?"

While her words were hanging there, right in midair, still a mere foot or two from her mouth, Betty shuddered all over in sock-shaking shock—as she suddenly realized that she had just asked a blabbermouth yak to...to answer a question!

Which meant that Betty would now likely be spending the next two days listening to Yackety yak and yak her unending answer.

"Hmmmm, why won't they listen?" began Yackety, clearing her throat. "Yes, yes, that's a very good question, which I'm sure must have a very good answer. Hmmmmm, let me see...," Yackety wondered out loud while she was thinking. Which is a very usual yak thing to do. "You say there was a group from Nhu Kaachu who wanted to save their village from being buried by an avalanche? Well, perhaps you could help save their village. Have you ever thought about that?"

Betty almost fell over—for two reasons. One, Yackety had answered her question in the unimaginably fewest words Betty the Yeti could ever recall. But! Two, her suggestion was actually brilliant!

However, when she went to agree with Yackety, all the wrong words came rushing out.

"Save Nhu Kaachu?" she growled. "Why should I? What have those mean Nhu Kaachuians ever done for me?"

For the first time in all the long, long time they had been friends, Yackety finally got angry and snorted at Betty. "Shame on you! You must always do the right thing simply because it's the right thing to do, dear. No matter what!" Yackety snorted. "You say the Kaachuians were mean to you once..."

"Yes!" Betty snorted right back. "They're mean, mean, mean!"

Yackety glared into Betty's eyes. "Just like you are, right now."

"I'm not being mean." Betty pouted petulantly. "I just

don't want to help them."

Yackety leaned closer until their noses were touching. "It's time to make up your mind—do you want to be angry for the rest of your life? Or would you rather begin being happy instead?"

And for the first time in all the long, long time they had been friends, Betty finally stopped arguing. She was too busy thinking instead. And at that exact moment in time, Betty the Yeti began to become a whole different yeti. Yackety's words stirred something hiding deep down inside—words that urged Betty to get on her lightning-like Icicle Built for Two. And to do what she knew she must do.

"Well, don't just stand there yakking all day." Betty very nearly smiled. "Saving Nhu Kaachu is the right thing for you to do, too. And I think I know just what to do. Let's go! I'll bet they're at The Hole Thing's hole right now!"

"The Hole Thing?" shuddered Yackety. "Why would they be there?"

"Because I tried to tell them how The Hole Thing is creating the avalanches," Betty said excitedly. "The big elf didn't believe me…but I think the little knight did."

Yackety looked nervously back at the woodpecker clock on the wall. "Oh dear, I hope it's not too late for us to help."

"You're right, Yackety! They're definitely going to need our help!" Betty bubbled with excitement. "Come on, Yackety, get out the lead—and rev up the sled! We have a village to save!"

11 The Great Wall of Ollie

Back down in the middle of The Mids, Sir Ollie stood with nervously knocking knees as Ghu's hideous hulk oozed ominously closer and closer. Little trickles of nervous perspiration ran from Sir Ollie's brow down into his eyes. Even Flit, his little flea friend on the end of his nose, was standing in a puddle up to his knees.

"Well, big brother, what're we gonna do now?" Flit said with a bit of a twitch. "We're trapped like two peas in a pod. With nowhere to go."

"I'm trying as hard as I can, but I just can't seem to think of a plan," was all that Sir Ollie could think of to say as Ghu edged closer still.

"Well, it's a good thing Ghu moves in slo mo," Flit said nervously, gaping into the glob's gaping mouth. "But keep working on that plan."

Ollie looked back up the long tunnel. "How much time have I got?"

"Ohhhhh, I'd say we've got about four minutes."

Although he tried as hard as he might, Sir Ollie still couldn't think of a single knightly way to win the day and defeat the slowly plodding glob of goo. Then he felt the hard stone wall up against his back and realized with a double-dry gulp that he had backed up as far as he could go.

But the moment his back touched that wall, Sir Ollie got the idea he was looking for.

And what a blindingly brilliant idea it was!

"A WALL!" he whooped, jumping for joy. "Flit, that's it! We need a...WALL! And you're the only one who can do it!"

"Me? Build a wall?" the little flea gasped in surprise. "Hey, take another look at me! I'm only a little white flea. I'm much, much too small to build much of a wall."

"I agree, you're only one little flea," Sir Ollie excitedly said. "But! You're also the wallah of a billion and three Snow Fleas, right?"

Flit was still confused. "Yeah. So?"

"So, little brother, if you have a billion and three Snow Fleas all working together—as one great big brother—you could build a wall thirty feet thick in less than three seconds," Sir Ollie encouraged him. "All you have to do is call all the Snow Fleas to gather together, and you'd have enough fleas to build a wall that runs all the way from Nhu Kaachu to Yubet, right?"

In a flash, Flit understood. "A wall! Right on, brother! I sure wish we'd thought of that a long time ago. Uh, but before we can get started, I'll need your help."

Sir Ollie pointed at himself. "Me?"

"Yep, yep, you. Here's what I want you to do."
Flit cupped his hands around his mouth and in a high-pitched sort of chant, he called out as loud as he could.

"To me, to me,
All fleas of the clan!
Come to me, brothers,
As quick as you can!"

Then Flit turned to Sir Ollie. "That's the rallying call of the Snow Fleas. Now I want you to shout that out as loud as you can because your voice is so much louder than mine. Otherwise, I'd have to run for miles in here to call the clan to a meeting."

Without even wondering what he was doing, Sir Ollie began bellowing Flit's rallying cry as loudly as he could...

"To me, to me,
All fleas of the clan!
Come to me, brothers,
As quick as you can!"

Then, from deep in the echoing orange gloom and from every direction, the porous, lava-rock walls of the tunnel seemed to come alive, slowly at first, then gaining momentum. From here and there and everywhere, the Snow Fleas were beginning to assemble.

"Louder!" Flit urged Sir Ollie.

"To me, to me, All fleas of the clan! Come to me, brothers, As quick as you can!"

And so from all the teeniest, tiniest holes, cracks, and crevices, billions of tiny fleas began to assemble.

They came through the walls. They came down from the ceiling. They even came up through the floor.

And before he could blink, Sir Ollie was suddenly up

to his knees in little white Snow Fleas—each one barely bigger than the period at the end of this sentence. He glanced quickly at the slow-moving mountain of goo. It was going to be close.

"Uh, we're down to a couple of minutes, little brother," Sir Ollie said. "Is this going to take long?"

As the clan assembled, Flit used the end of Sir Ollie's nose as his stage. "Listen up, brothers, one and all," Flit addressed them as loudly as he could, as more little critters continued to pour in from every direction. "I want you to meet our new friend, Sir Ollie Everghettz, a Mighty Knight from a faraway land, who came here to help us and Queen Elynor."

Flit's speech was immediately interrupted by a rousing round of applause, then he continued.

"It seems we have a little problem. Yep, yep, you guessed it. Once again, Ghu wants to have us for dinner. But this time, Sir Ollie has come up with a perfect plan...

if we all work together as brothers, we can finally stop Ghu. Not just for now, but for ever! Because when we all work together, we Snow Fleas can do anything!"

This was met by another rousing round of applause.

"A minute and a half," Sir Ollie reminded him. "How about a little less talk and a lot more action!"

"Hey, I'm just gettin' started!" Flit snorted. "So what we're gonna do, brothers one and all, we're gonna build a solid WALL of Snow Fleas between us and Ghu— and for once and for ever, we'll show Ghu just who The Mids belong to!"

The whistling and cheering that followed was almost deafening—if you were a flea.

"And when the wall is finished, little brothers, we're gonna call it...The Great Wall of Ollie!"

"I love it!" Sir Ollie said frantically. "Now, let's get building!"

Without the need for any further orders, the still-gathering Snow Fleas began forming a solid wall of fleas—with arms joining arms and legs joining legs—between the looming glob of Ghu and Sir Ollie.

"You're doin' just fine, brothers! Keep up the good work," Flit encouraged them from the end of Sir Ollie's nose, as he anxiously glanced at Ghu's wide-open mouth oozing closer and closer.

"Less than a minute!" Sir Ollie reminded them. "Go! Go! Go! And when you've finished building The Great Wall of Ollie, we've got to get down to Nhu Kaachu to warn the villagers that an avalanche is coming."

Immediately, all the fleas stopped working and stared over at Flit.

"Why are you stopping?" Sir Ollie shouted as loudly as he could. "Don't stop now! Ghu's almost on top of us."

One little flea flew up and landed beside Flit on the end of Sir Ollie's nose. "Why should we help the Kaachuians?"

"Because they need help," Sir Ollie gasped.

"But why should we help them? They're no friends of ours, that's for sure!" About a billion other Snow Fleas all agreed. "Every time we go in to Nhu Kaachu for a bite to eat and a friendly 'hello,' all they do is whap us and slap us and spray bug spray in our face..."

"And thwack us with swatters!" another flea added.

"And look what the Nhu Kaachuians did to Betty," someone else said, snorting. "They bullied her and teased her and called her awful names. Why should we help people like that! C'mon, everyone, let's go home."

As billions of the little fleas turned to head home, the once Great Wall of Ollie quickly began to crumble and tumble down all around them.

"Wait!" Sir Ollie called out before he knew what he was going to say.

Most of the Snow Fleas stopped what they were doing but didn't turn around.

Then the answer came to him in a flash. "I know a way everyone can be friends."

The little fleas all turned around.

"How can we do that, brother?" Flit wanted to know.

"Tell 'em the truth! Tell 'em that Snow Fleas are called Snow Fleas because the only thing Snow Fleas eat is snow!" Sir Ollie reminded them. "But, y'see, the Nhu Kaachuians don't know that. They think you're gonna bite them, like fleas on a dog. That's why they swat you and thwack you."

There was a long—a very long—pause while all the Snow Fleas thought about Sir Ollie's thought.

"Yeah, maybe you're right," one of them finally said. "I always thought they swatted and thwacked us because they didn't like us."

"You're right. Maybe we should give the Kaachuians one last chance," said another.

"Yeah, let's try being friends for a change," another flea agreed. "But remember, just one little thwack—and this friendship is over. Forever."

"We can worry about that later," Flit excitedly suggested. "Now, c'mon, everyone, let's get going. We've got a Great Wall to build!"

Then, all at once, the little Snow Fleas immediately rejoined their arms and legs and finished the Great Wall of Ollie—and just in the nick of time, too.

From the other side of The Great Wall, Ghu let out an agonized Ghu roar that sounded a lot like a balloon does when you blow one up and let it go.

Sir Ollie looked cross-eyed at Flit. "Whoo! You did it! We're almost good to go! But, uh, there's just one more little thing..."

Grinning from ear to ear, Flit turned back to Sir Ollie. "Yeah? What's that?"

Ollie put his hand on the solid wall of rocks behind them. "Well, we still have to get past this wall behind us. D'you think you could sorta get your flea friends to make a hole in the wall—so we can get out of here?"

Flit's grin grew even bigger. "Hey, no problem, brother. I bet we can handle this. Watch this." He put two fingers up to his mouth and whistled shrilly, then called to the Snow Flea foreman. "Uh, Gnosh, could I see you over here, quick?"

"Sure, boss, what's up?" Gnosh eagerly asked.

Flit pointed to the wall of rocks Ghu's boulder had created. "Sir Ollie and I have to get down to Nhu Kaachu! Can you get a crew to move this pile of rocks out of the way?"

"I'm on it!" came the instant reply. "You'll be on your way before you can say 'What wall?'" The little flea grinned, then called out, "Uh, could I have a million or so fleas over here ASAP!"

Flit turned back to Sir Ollie. "Hey, we can call this project The Great Hole of Ollie!"

12 Sir Seth Thwacks & Thwarts the Thing

High up the mountain, Sir Seth and Shasta were courageously crawling back up to the wide-open mouth of The Hole Thing's cave—to try to sneak a quick peek inside.

The Hole Thing had not only pushed a huge new boulder up to the opening, he had already gone back to get another.

Elynor quietly appeared beside them.

"Oh no, he's beginning to block up the entrance all over again," Sir Seth whispered, slumping down in the snow.

Elynor slumped down beside him. "What are we going to do now?"

"I'm working on it," Sir Seth said, thinking quickly. "Let's see now, my sword's way too small to slow him down at all. And my lance isn't much better..."

Elynor looked at him nervously. "That doesn't leave us much to work with, does it?"

"No," Sir Seth had to admit. "Just lots and lots of snow."

And that's when Shasta leaped to the rescue! She suddenly began rolling a snowball with her nose, barking excitedly.

"Not now, Shasta," Sir Seth grumped, deep in thought.

"There'll be time to play later. Right now, we have a pressing Mighty Knightly problem to solve."

But Shasta persisted. She rolled the snowball right up to Sir Seth's hand, excitedly jumping and barking as loudly as she could.

"Wait! I think Shasta's trying to tell you something," Elynor said, sitting up.

Just as Sir Seth began to understand what Shasta was trying to say, suddenly, from out of nowhere...

WHAP!

A long snaky blue feeler lashed out from inside The Hole, missing Sir Seth's ear by less than an inch. However, like the fearless and unflinching Mighty Knight that he was, Sir Seth Thistlethwaite instinctively swept into action.

"It's The Thing's feelers—feeling around for our brains again!" he called out. "Quickly, m'lady, man the cannons!"

"Cannons? What cannons?" Elynor wondered out loud, looking around.

"The ones that launch the nice, icy Thistle Missiles!" Sir Seth crowed victoriously, patting Shasta on the head. "Good thinking, girl! Why didn't I think of that?"

"What's a...Thistle Missile?"

"THIS...is a Thistle Missile," Sir Seth said excitedly. And with that, he reached down and scooped up a huge handful of snow, then began packing a thick, icy Thistle Missile—which is a cannonball you make from snow that you pack twice as long and three times as hard as an ordinary snowball. But you probably already knew that.

Then, when his nice, icy Thistle Missile was rock hard and ready, he took careful aim and fired it into the cave as hard as he could.

There was a slight pause, followed by a fearsome, mighty roar.

"HEY! KNOCK IT OFF, WILLYUH!"

"BULLSEYE!" Sir Seth said excitedly. "Okay, m'lady, now let's give him a full 21-gun barrage!"

Watching Sir Seth in utter amazement, Elynor quickly scooped up a large handful of snow and began packing a snowball for the first time ever, just as Sir Seth was finishing his second Thistle Missile. Then his third, fourth, fifth, and fifteenth. When they had made another two dozen, Sir Seth turned to her with a huge smile.

"Ready, m'lady?"

"Ready!" she said with a huge happy grin.

"Then...FIRE!"

Immediately, a 21-gun broadside barrage of thick, icy Thistle Missiles filled the frosty air. And from inside the cave, The Hole Thing let out a mighty roar as the barrage exploded in a feeler-freezing salvo all over his already frigid blue face. And down his wide-open and getting-ready-to-roar throat!

"Okay, quickly, your highness...RELOAD!"

As they were preparing another salvo, from inside the cave The Hole Thing let out a not-quite-so-mighty roar.

"OH NO! WHAT'S HAPPENING TO ME!"

Sir Seth noticed The Thing's roar was getting weaker. And smaller. He quickly turned to Elynor. "Something really strange is happening here. Quickly, m'lady, let's hit him with another barrage!"

They made more icy Thistle Missiles as thick and fast as their hands could pack them. Then, this time, it was Elynor who called out...

"FIRE!"

There was another slight pause, followed by another not-nearly-as-mighty roar as the not-nearly-as-mighty roar from before.

"WHAT HAVE YOU DONE!"

Sir Seth couldn't stand the suspense one minute longer. "C'mon, everyone, let's get in there and see what's happening!"

Shasta's excited barking echoed off all the walls for more than two minutes as she jumped down to the floor of the cave and went running around with her nose to the ground, anxiously looking for something blue to bite.

"It's...awfully quiet in here," Elynor whispered, also looking all around.

"Fear not!" Sir Seth smiled Mighty Knightfully, swinging his sword from side to side. "We have my trusty steed and my sword to protect us!"

Then he cautiously took two steps into The Hole, then paused and called out, "Um, yoo hoo, Mister Thing? I was wondering if we could have a little chat."

If The Hole Thing heard him, it didn't say a single Thing thing.

So Sir Seth kept going. "We were, uh, y'know, sorta wondering if maybe you'd like to find a new place to live. Like, uh, somewhere a little bit warmer."

Still, The Thing didn't say a thing.

Seth turned to Elynor. "He must have gone way back into the cave...," he started to say, but Shasta's sudden, frantic barking stopped him in the middle of his sentence.

"Look! What's that?" Elynor said as she knelt down on one knee and picked something up from the floor.

Sir Seth looked over her shoulder. "What is it?"

Elynor held her hand down so he could see. "It's The Hole Thing! And look, he's only one inch long!"

Sir Seth couldn't believe his eyes. The snowballs had shrunk the once-fearsome Hole Thing from a towering tyrannosaurus rex down to a dew worm.

"What...have you done to me?" a little voice cried out.

"The Thistle Missiles must have shrunk him!" Sir Seth gasped, holding Shasta back. "So that's why he wanted to block up The Hole. Not to keep out the cold—but because he didn't want the snow to shrink him!"

"Right," Elynor gasped, still too shocked to talk.

Sir Seth looked up at Elynor's gentle face. "So...what do we do now?"

"I've got an idea," Sir Seth said, taking the little 'pillar from her hand. "I'm gonna put him in my coat pocket until we get back down to the bottom of the mountain." He smiled over one shoulder, as he boosted Shasta back out through the opening of the cave. "Then we can put him somewhere he won't bother anyone, like in Public School Number Two in old Kaachu."

"At the bottom of the mountain! Oh, Sir Seth, what a wonderful idea! That solves the whole problem!" She smiled back. "Without The Thing up here, that means The Hole will remain open forever and ever and ever."

"And that means no more avalanches forever and ever and ever."

Sir Seth reached up to help Elynor. "That's right!" He grinned triumphantly. "C'mon, give me your hand. We've got to get out of here and find Betty..."

Elynor was still excitedly jumping for joy when—in a spray of freshly schussing snow—Betty the Yeti and Yackety suddenly arrived, catching everyone completely by surprise. As the lightning-fast sled slid to a snowy stop, Elynor automatically took two steps back the minute she saw Betty the Yeti.

"Don't worry. We came here to help you!" Betty shouted with a huge, happy grin. But when she looked into Elynor's eyes, her enthusiasm instantly cooled.

"Help? From a yeti?" Elynor said icily. "I don't think so."

But Sir Seth instantly went over and stood beside Betty. "She came a long way to help us. I think we should hear what she has to say."

"Why do we need her?" Elynor continued coldly. "Shasta helped us solve The Hole Thing problem."

"HAH!" Betty snorted just like the beastly Betty of old. "The Hole Thing is only HALF your problem!"

"Half?" Sir Seth said.

Betty pointed a long bony finger down the mountain. "Yes, half! You seem to be forgetting there's an ENORMOUS avalanche building up down there—and it's about to bury Nhu Kaachu. I can take you down there on my icicle sled in time to save the village. If you'll just let me."

"No!" Elynor snorted.

"Why not?" Sir Seth gasped. "It's the fastest way down the mountain!"

"I still don't trust Betty the Yeti," Elynor said simply. "And neither should you."

"Oh, but you can trust her!" Sir Seth insisted, challenging the queen. "And I know just how you can do it." He reached down and grabbed a handful of snow, then held it up to Elynor. "Here, share some snow with her right here and now—enter her mind. And find out for yourself."

"You want me to share snow? With Betty the Yeti?" Elynor gasped.

"She may be a yeti on the outside," Sir Seth reminded her. "But she's just Betty on the inside."

When she heard Sir Seth's wise words, Elynor knew he was right. "Quickly, everyone. Sit down."

The five of them sat down in a circle and passed each other a handful of snow. Immediately, Elynor was jolted by the shimmering dreamscapes she sensed in Betty's mind. She felt Betty's anger and her deeply hurt feelings. Her loneliness. Disappointment. And the deep, enduring sadness around her great big broken heart.

For a brief moment, Elynor also caught blurred glimpses of Betty's first day at school and felt the hurt that Betty felt as she saw the children's laughing faces. And above everything else, she heard their cruel, hurtful words echoing in her mind...It's King Kong! It's a yucky yeti!! We're all going to die!!

Elynor suddenly sagged with shame.

"I have seen all I need to know," Elynor said sadly and put her hand on one of Betty's huge paws. "Betty, I owe you an enormous apology. And so does all of Ah Ah Kaachu...," she said as another tremendous tremor shook the entire mountain.

Then—as they all watched in horror—the rest of the overhanging ledge of snow suddenly slid past The Hole Thing's hole. It began thundering down the side of the mountain, heading straight for The Flats and gathering more and more snow as it went.

Betty gaped in open-mouthed awe. "Oh no! This time there's much too much snow. The Flats will overflow and start an avalanche for sure!"

Time was finally running out.

Which meant that no one in Nhu Kaachu would ever know that Betty the Yeti had tried to do something nice for someone once.

"Come on, everybody, it's still not too late," Betty insisted, springing into action. "Get on my sled! NOW!"

13 Flit's Super Surprise

Deep within The Mids, Sir Ollie and a few hundred thousand Snow Fleas moved the very last of the lava rocks out of the way, then looked back up at The Great Wall of Ollie. It ominously bulged and ballooned as Ghu did his evil, level best to bash and batter his way through, but so far, the wall of arm-in-arm Snow Fleas was holding solidly together.

"Hey, we did it, brother." Sir Ollie grinned from ear to ear. "We stopped him!"

"Well, for now anyhow," Flit agreed with a grin. "Of course, the boys'll have to work out an Ollie Wall schedule among themselves—to make sure Ghu stays out. But c'mon, right now, we gotta get down to Nhu Kaachu."

With one eye still on the dangerously bashing and thrashing bulge in the wall, Sir Ollie slid El Gonzo back into his belt. "Okay, but uh, are you sure those little guys are tough enough to keep Ghu out?"

"Hey, you don't have to be big to be tough, y'know!" Flit said with a grin.

Sir Ollie broke into a great big grin of his own. "Right. All you gotta be is tough."

"Right! And when you're fightin' for what you believe is right, my guys are extra tough, each and every one of them." Flit's great big grin grew even bigger. "Now, c'mon. I've got another little Snow Flea surprise waiting for you, brother. See The Mighty Wall of Ollie over there?"

"What about it?" Sir Ollie wondered worriedly. "I hope there's an elevator back there."

"Not quite. But it seems to me, if a few billion fleas can build a wall tough enough to stop Ghu...then building something as simple as a Snow Flea Sled should be a snap."

Sir Ollie went cross-eyed, looking at Flit. "A what?"

The little flea ran as fast as he could and slid up to the bridge of Sir Ollie's nose. "I said, a Snow Flea Sled, brother!" Flit shouted a little bit louder—which, really, wasn't much louder at all. "Haven't you heard? It's the new way to get around town, and the best way to zip down to Nhu Kaachu."

Sir Ollie was so excited, he started to run down the tunnel. "Whoo! A sled made from Snow Fleas? Hey, that's too neat to be true. Where is it, little brother?"

Flit ran back to the end of Sir Ollie's nose and pointed down the tunnel. "There's a way out about ten minutes from here—called Doorway 22. By the time we get there, your flea sled will be waiting outside. And you're gonna love it!"

"Sounds good to me. Let's move out!" Sir Ollie said as he instantly took off down the long eerie tunnel.

They hadn't gone far when Sir Ollie went cross-eyed

and asked, "Where does this orange lava light come from?"

"Oh that?" Flit called over one shoulder. "Y'see, this mountain used to be a volcano a long time ago. But now, whenever the lava erupts, it only comes up as far as the bottom of the mountain. Then it kinda bubbles and boils for a while before it un-erupts and goes back down into the ground. But while the lava's here, that's how the Firefleas get their light—and how The Mids gets its heat."

"Firefleas? What's a..."

"Fireflea?" Flit finished Sir Ollie's question. "It's a Snow Flea that stores the light from the lava, then releases it slowly. They're all over The Mids. That's what this light really is—billions of firefleas giving off lava light."

Sir Ollie looked up all around the roof of the tunnel. "And that's where all the light in here comes from?"

"Yep. Why do you ask?"

Sir Ollie's Mighty Knight mind was whirling as fast as the wheels on his bike. "Oh, stuff like that's always good to know, y'know, in case you need it, sometime. Like, for example, whenever you have another problem with Ghu, you can tell all the Firefleas to turn off the lights—and leave him stumblin' and bumblin' around in the dark."

Flit turned around with a big grin. "Hey, brilliant, big brother. That's somethin' else we should have thought of a long time ago..."

But Sir Ollie suddenly interrupted and changed the

subject. "Oh, I think I see sunlight up ahead. Does that mean we've reached the next entrance?"

"Yep, we're at Doorway 22. And your Snow Flea Sled, too," Flit said in his usual, bubbly way. "So, get ready, brother. When you rev up that sled, you're gonna make lightning look slow."

As they reached the narrow overhead opening, Flit pointed to the wall. "There's some stairs over there."

Sir Ollie scrambled up the well-worn stone steps and crawled out into the instantly double-dazzling sunlight and snow. It was so glinty and squinty and dazzlingly bright, he couldn't see a thing for almost a minute. Then, slowly, little by little, he began to focus. And there it was, in all its magnificent, heart-grabbing glory...

A streamlined Snow Flea Sled, ready to go!

It was the most sensationally streamlined sled that he'd ever laid eyes on. It was white as winter all over, from the tip of its rocket-ship-shaped nose to the end of its sleek Snow Flea–shaped body, with a large number "1" embossed on the hood. Sir Ollie couldn't wait to get in and get going.

"Ohhhhh, Flit!" Sir Ollie finally found the words, "This is just too neat to be true!"

Flit was so proud of all of the Snow Fleas, he would have popped all the buttons off his shirt—if he'd been wearing a shirt with buttons to pop.

"Hey, hey, Snow Fleas! Are we ready to roll?!"

All the fleas excitedly shouted back at the tops of their

lungs, imitating the sound of a red-hot dragster. "Vroom, vroom, VROOM! Burgle, burgle, pop, pop, pop. C'mon, you guys, let's go!"

Flit turned to Sir Ollie and held out one arm. "Okay, Sir Ollie, hop in. Let's take Snow Flea Sled Number One for a quick little spin...down to Nhu Kaachu."

"Whoa! Wait a minute! Did you hear that?" Flit called to all the fleas, looking with wide-eyed worry at the gathering storm clouds at the top of the mountain. "Oh, oh. The snow has started to flow from The Hole Thing's hole down to The Flats! And you know what that means..."

"Vroom, vroom, VROOM!" all the fleas forming the Snow Flea Sled called out as one. "C'mon, hop on, we gotta get down to Nhu Kaachu!"

Flit had about six seconds to make up his madly whirling mind. Was there enough time to beat the avalanche down to Nhu Kaachu? Maybe yes. Maybe no.

"Well, little buddy, what do you think?" Sir Ollie asked, also looking up at the thundering tons of slowly sliding snow. "Can we do it?"

"Hard to say, brother. It's gonna be close." Flit calculated quickly. "Let's see, it'll take all that snow about ten minutes to get to The Flats...then about ten minutes more to begin building up...and about two more minutes to..."

"It doesn't matter," Sir Ollie cut him off as he scurried over to the waiting sled. "We've got to get down there and warn Nhu Kaachu! No matter what."

He slipped into the streamlined cockpit of the sleek Snow Flea Sled and hunched down behind the hood with the embossed number "1" and instantly felt right at home. There was even a speedometer on the dashboard, just like the one in his dad's car.

Sir Ollie gripped the steering wheel and looked cross-eyed at Flit. "Uh, have you got the key?"

"Key? You gotta be kidding, brother. With a Snow Flea Sled, all you have to do is say...GO!"

The minute they heard the word "GO," all the Snow Fleas began running as fast as they could on their billions and billions of flying flea legs. Then, in about three seconds flat, they lifted their legs and the sled began to slide, slowly at first, then faster and faster, until Sir Ollie and Flit were approaching warp speed, heading straight for the village of Nhu Kaachu.

"Uh...Flit?"

"Yep?" the little flea asked over one shoulder.

"Um...how fast d'you think we're going?"

"Ohhhhh, I don't know, I think we're approaching Warp One. Why do you ask?"

Sir Ollie looked frantically, everywhere on the floor in front of him. "Well, I can't seem to find a brake pedal. When we get to Nhu Kaachu, how are we gonna stop?"

Flit thought about it quickly. "Uh, good question."

Sir Ollie began to get nervous. "You mean, you don't know how to stop?"

"Awwww, don't worry about it. We'll think of somethin'."

14 A Race to the Finish!

Meanwhile, back up at the mouth of The Hole Thing's hole, Betty led the charge to get on her blindingly-fast Icicle Built for Two. All around them, a final, hunormous feeder was rampaging down the mountain toward the slippy, tippy tons of snow piled precariously on The Flats.

"C'mon, everyone, here we goooo!" Betty called over one shoulder.

"And remember, we must keep going, Betty—no matter what!" Yackety said. "If you don't do something nice now, you'll always be known as the same old beastly Betty the Yeti!"

Sir Seth yelled back. "We can talk about that later. Right now, let's go. Go. GO!"

"You're right, Betty," Elynor cried. "Now it's all up to you. It's gonna be close but it's gotta be done."

Betty the Yeti pointed the sled runners straight down the mountain and in a puff of fluffy snow, they were suddenly off and on their way. Picking up blinding speed, they flew past The Flats...and headed down the steep sheer face of Kill Hill. But Betty was a pro, cool and calm.

She shouted over one shoulder to Sir Seth. "That's Yackety Yak, my only friend in the whole world, behind you."

Sir Seth just shook Yackety by her one furry foot and

bellowed into Betty's ear, "Thank you for coming here to help us! I know this wasn't an easy decision for you to make."

At first, Betty said nothing. Then she patted Sir Seth on one hand. "I would never have done it if it hadn't been for you."

"Me? What do you mean?"

Betty swerved to avoid a snagglefoot tree. "It was something you did the first time I met you."

Sir Seth could feel his cheeks turning red. "Yeah? What did I do?"

"You and your other knight friend are the first people I've ever met who actually...listened to me!"

Now it was Sir Seth's turn to pat Betty's hand. "And you just proved we were right."

"How did you know what was going on in my mind?"

"Call it a hunch," he said. "Besides, one of the rules in the Mighty Knights Book of Right & Honor says, 'What you see on the outside is what someone looks like. What you find on the inside is what that person is like.'"

Betty thought about that as long as she could. "Thank you, Sir Seth," she finally said. "Whether we save Nhu Kaachu or not, at least I know in my heart that we tried."

At that exact moment, Sir Seth glanced anxiously over one shoulder—just as tons upon tons of thundering snow finally spilled over the edge of The Flats and began rumbling down the side of the mountain, slowly picking up speed, heading straight for Nhu Kaachu.

The race to save Nhu Kaachu was truly on!

"The Flats just overflowed!" Sir Seth frantically warned everyone. "Oh boy, you better floor this thing, Betty. This is gonna be close."

Instinctively, all five of them leaned forward as far as they could, hoping to coax just one more mile per hour from the plummeting sled, when suddenly, they ran smack into a patch of fully stretched slingshot shrubs lurking just below the snow.

"W-w-what's happening?" Sir Seth shouted with shock. "We're slowing down!"

"Sorry, Sir Seth, I didn't see..."

But Betty didn't have time to finish saying "all those fully stretched slingshot shrubs lurking under the snow" before all those slingshot shrubs lurking under the snow suddenly snagged the speedily schussing sled and shot it halfway back up the mountain—depositing everyone in a panicky pile of paws, knees, and noses under five feet of snow and the heavy icicle sled—directly in the path of the HUNORMOUS onrushing avalanche.

Sir Seth frantically felt around under the snow until he finally found Shasta. "C'mon, girl, hurry! We gotta get everyone out from under all this!"

Shasta instantly jumped into action. She furiously began digging down, sending the snow flying in all directions with all four paws at once. Which is something few other horses can do.

First, she came upon Yackety, who was already feeling around for Betty, as Sir Seth helped Elynor up and felt around inside his coat pocket to make sure The Hole Thing was still there.

Without another word and with a Mighty Knightly heave, Sir Seth reached down and instantly righted the big sled all by himself. And when he turned around, everyone was waiting and ready to go.

"C'mon, everyone, there's still time! We're off to Nhu Kaachu!"

No one had to be asked twice. In about two
seconds flat, everyone dove onto the sled in a
whole new tumbling tangle of knees and noses,
arms, paws, and toeses as though it were
an Olympic bobsled event. And with that,
Sir Seth and his band of unusual friends
clambered onto Betty's icicle sled
and pushed off all over again.

At first, they managed to keep just ahead of the fast-flowing snow, but little by little, the avalanche began picking up speed...until it was a rumbling, tumbling tower of snow looming four feet behind them.

"It's gaining on us!" Yackety yelled over the roaring rush of the runners on the snow. "Faster! We've got to go faster!"

"We're already going faster!" Betty called back desperately. "We can't go any faster than that!"

Sir Seth anxiously peered over one shoulder at the onrushing mountain of snow. "Oh no! It's not fast enough. What're we gonna do..."

But the mountain had already made up their minds for them.

Before anyone knew what had happened, Betty's streaking ice sled suddenly sped up, over and off a long large ledge lurking like a ski jump just below the surface—and took off like a rocket in a slow-motion explosion of snow.

And from high overhead and still upside down, they all watched as the avalanche swept by below them!

Poor Old Nhu Kaachu

Luckily, Sir Seth and Shasta landed lightly, downside up, in a cushioning bank of soft fluffy snow. Sir Seth picked himself up and ran over to Elynor, who was standing beside the big brass bell on top of Nhu Kaachu Public School Number Two—which was the only way you now even knew you were in Nhu Kaachu. Because the entire village had been buried beneath forty-two feet of fresh, still-settling snow.

"Oh no," Sir Seth gasped, kneeling down by the bell.

"Why are you so worried about an old brass bell?" Yackety grinned, trying to cheer him up.

"Because it's on top of Nhu Kaachu Public School Number Two," Elynor sighed sadly, taking Yackety by the hand. Well, make that a hoof.

"Oh!" she whispered. "You mean, there's a school under here?"

"Yes," was all Elynor was able to say before she slumped down. "And the entire village of Nhu Kaachu is under there, too. Oh dear, deary me, if only I had listened to Betty the Yeti when she was trying to tell me about The Hole Thing, all this would never have happened..."

Yackety was so sad and upset she couldn't think of a single thing to say. So the four of them sat there in the silence of the snow, sadly thinking their own sorrowful thoughts.

"Um, where's Betty?" Sir Seth finally wondered, trying to think of something new to say. "Have you seen her?"

Oh no! OH NO!

While his words were still in midair, Sir Seth suddenly realized he had just made the mistake of asking a yak a question. Yackety delightedly began endlessly answering. "Yes, well I'm so glad you asked. I don't see her here anywhere...or over there either. Perhaps I should go have a look up there. Yes, that's what I'll do. You stay here and I'll..."

But just then, from somewhere on the other side of a huge hill of snow, there suddenly came the hubbub of hundreds of happily bubbling voices. Sir Seth sat up and looked all around, stunned and surprised. Shasta also perked up and ran to the top of the pile for a peek.

"What's that?" he asked a yak another question before Yackety had a chance to fully answer the first. But Yackety was so excited, she didn't notice.

"It sounds like…voices to me," Elynor said, double delightedly. "Make that lots and lots and lots of happy voices!" she added just as Mayor Mae Knott came into view, followed by the entire population of Nhu Kaachu.

Shasta began jumping for joy and ran, barking excitedly, to the top of the huge pile of snow, and disappeared out of sight. Then, from the other side of the snow, everyone heard a voice they hadn't heard for a Mighty Knightly long time…

"Hey, put me down, brothers, I've gotta find my friend, Sir Seth—the other Mighty Knight!"

Sir Seth immediately jumped to his feet. "By golly! It's Sir Ollie!"

Then, as though it had all been rehearsed, Sir Ollie's grinning face appeared above the hill of snow, shortly followed by all of the rest of Sir Ollie being carried on the shoulders of two thousand and two cheering Nhu Kaachuian villagers. Who, in turn, were being carried on the shoulders of a billion and three cheering Snow Fleas.

The only thing missing was a high school marching band with bugles and banners, which the Snow Fleas would have gladly provided—if only they had known what a marching band was.

When Sir Ollie saw Sir Seth running toward him, he jumped down from the villagers' shoulders and ran over to his long-lost friend, bubbling and babbling as fast as his lips would go.

"Sir Seth, Sir Seth! You're not gonna buhhhhh-lieve where I've been!" he shouted excitedly and began telling him his entire side of the story. "I've been in the middle of The Mids! Fighting this huge green slimeball called Ghu..."

"Oh? Is that all?" Sir Seth pretended to yawn. "Well, while you were playing around with a little glop of goo, Shasta and I were up at the top of the mountain in The Hole Thing's hole fighting a giant killer 'pillar..."

"A what!"

"Oh, nothin' much. Just a giant killer caterpillar with feelers fifty feet long that suck the brains right outta your head!" Then he leaned closer. "Hey, what's that on the end of your nose?"

Now it was Sir Ollie's turn to fake a yawn. "Oh, that's my buddy Flit, the wallah of the Snow Fleas."

"The what?"

"The wallah. What's the matter, you never heard of a wallah?"

"What's a wallah?"

"Hey, other brother, good to meetcha." Flit grinned, clearing his throat. "A wallah's what you might call the mayor of the mountain and..."

But Sir Ollie excitedly interrupted, "Flit got all the Snow Fleas to sorta glom together and make this lightning-like rocket sled that I rode...with a for-real avalanche about three inches behind me all the way down the mountain!"

"Like, double ho hum!" bragged Sir Seth. "I met a snowshoe elf...who's the Faerie Queen of all of Ah Ah Kaachu! How about that!"

Sir Ollie waved to Elynor. "Uh, Sir Seth? You mean my Inside-My-Mind Friend, Elynor, who makes snow taste like a butterscotch sundae?"

Just then, in the middle of all the excitement, the entire mountain shuddered and shook ominously all over again.

"Oh no! Run, everyone!" all the villagers screamed, "There's another avalanche coming!"

"It's okay. Stay where you are." Sir Ollie smiled proudly. "It's not another avalanche. What you hear is Ghu trying to break through the wall of Snow Fleas and get back into The Mids."

"Goo? Snow Fleas?" Sir Seth wondered out loud. "What are you babbling about?"

Sir Ollie's grin grew even more. "It's a looooong story.

I'll tell you later."

"It's so good to see you are safe, Sir Ollie," Elynor said happily as she walked over to join them.

"Uh, hi, your highness." Sir Ollie grinned. "Good to see you, too."

"How did you manage to get to Nhu Kaachu before the avalanche?" she asked.

"Well, it wasn't easy," Sir Ollie began modestly, then took a deep breath. "But like I said, my buddy Flit here got all his Snow Flea friends together and they made this super-fast sled and we started down to Nhu Kaachu just as the snow overflowed on The Flats—and, uh, chased us all the way down here to Nhu Kaachu. But we got here just in the nick of time to warn everyone. It was really, really close..."

"But we did it!" Flit enthusiastically finished Sir Ollie's sentence.

However, the triumph wasn't over yet.

"Oh, no! Look who's coming," somebody suddenly said somberly.

All one billion and three cheering fleas and two thousand and two villagers turned to look. And there was Betty the Yeti standing forlornly on the side of the mountain. With Yackety standing beside her.

"It's Betty the Yeti! Get her! This is our chance to get rid of her for good!" everyone else said when they saw her.

Everyone except for Sir Seth, that is, who was the

only one who said, "Why?"

"Why?" one of the villagers sneered snidely.
"What do you mean by 'why'? That's Betty the
Yeti! She caused all this..."

"No! Betty did not make this happen!" Elynor said
firmly, stepping up to the top of the snow. "But I know
who did! Thanks to these valiant Mighty Knights, Sir
Seth and Sir Ollie—and their trusty steed, Shasta—who
risked their lives to come here to help us, I now have an
important announcement to make. But before I begin, I
want Betty the Yeti to come down here to hear what
I have to say."

The Kaachuians mumbled and grumbled, not knowing
what Elynor meant.

Betty the Yeti stood staring down at the villagers
staring up at her. When she saw Sir Seth, she gave him
a shy wave of her hand with her arm still by her side.

It happened so quickly that even Mayor Mae Knott may or may not have noticed. Betty was obviously trying to decide what to do, but Elynor helped her make up her mind.

"Betty!" Elynor called out. "Please come down here and join us. I have an important announcement I want everyone here to hear."

"I can hear you from here!" came Betty's defensive reply.

"No, no, please come down here!" Elynor repeated. "I promise you, you will be glad that you did."

Betty took three unsure steps, remembered the last time she had trusted the Kaachuians, then stopped and stared.

"Very well, if you prefer, you can listen from there," Elynor called out. "Ladies and gentlemen of Nhu Kaachu, I have wonderful news to tell you this day! For thousands of years, this mighty mountain has stood here without a name—as Kaachuians, everywhere, waited for that most memorable day when a true Kaachuian hero would come along to give the mountain its name!"

A ripple of excitement ran through the throngs of expectant Nhu Kaachuians.

"I bet she's gonna call it Mount Sir Seth," one villager whispered.

"Nawwww, it's gotta be Mount Sir Ollie," said another. "He saved the village, not Sir Seth."

"No way," said a third. "It has to be the Mighty Knights Mountain."

But Elynor surprised them all, including Sir Seth and Sir Ollie.

"Ladies and gentlemen of Nhu Kaachu, it gives me great pleasure to officially present to you...
MOUNT BETTY!"

Immediately, fifty-five villagers fainted, eleven fell violently ill, and ninety-two had to be treated for shock. Even Betty the Yeti slipped off the edge of her sled. But no one said a word.

"And I'm sure you want to know why!" Elynor

continued. "Well, thanks to our two courageous Mighty Knights, I've discovered that the problem has been The Hole Thing! Not Betty!"

"Aha! Didn't I tell you!" one villager knowingly nudged his neighbor. "I knew it was The Hole Thing the whole time!"

"Of course!" another snorted just a little bit louder. "Who else could it have been?"

"Yes, yes, yes. I've always said The Hole Thing has such sneaky eyes." The snorting continued all through the crowd.

Elynor then went on to explain the whole thing about The Hole Thing in complete detail and when she was finished, all the Nhu Kaachuians looked up the hill, almost afraid to see what Betty's reaction would be.

"Betty, everyone in Nhu Kaachu owes you an apology," Elynor concluded. "Please come down here and join us, my friend. I promise, you will never be ridiculed, ever again."

Then she turned to face the Mighty Knights. "And to you, Sir Seth and Sir Ollie..."

"Woo woo woo," Shasta interrupted.

"Oh yes, and to you, too, Shasta. Thank you for helping me get to know all of my kingdom. And all of the people in it." She smiled down at Flit, then looked up at Betty. "Oh! I almost forgot! What are we going to do with The Hole Thing?" She turned to Sir Seth. "Is he still in your pocket?"

Sir Seth felt around inside his coat pocket—but The Hole Thing was gone! "Oh no! He must have fallen out when I landed upside down."

"Now what are we going to do?" she wondered, looking all around.

"I don't know." Sir Seth shrugged. "But he'll probably stay shrunk forever in all of this snow. If he ever becomes a problem all over again, though, Sir Ollie and Shasta and I will be glad to come back here—to help you out all over again."

Immediately, two thousand and two villagers' voices let out a great cheer—followed by a billion and three Snow Fleas cheering even louder.

And so, all of the Snow Fleas and Nhu Kaachuians (and yaks and yetis) lived happily ever after and rebuilt the village of Nhu Nhu Kaachu safely at the bottom of the mountain.

And as far as Sir Seth and Sir Ollie have been able to find out, there hasn't been another avalanche there since they left Ah Ah Kaachu. Or a Hole Thing either. As far as they know...

EPILOGUE
The Mists of Moro

Elynor took Sir Seth and Sir Ollie by the hand and, with a large tearful lump in her throat, managed to say: "Thank you for coming. And thank you for all you did while you were here. Ah Ah Kaachu can't thank you enough!"

"We had a ton of fun, your highness," Sir Seth said, "but now it's time to get back to Thatchwych. And home."

"Have a safe journey, everyone..."

"Thank you, your highness, we will." Sir Seth grinned.

But then a sudden frown clouded Elynor's serene face. "Oh, and whatever you do, be sure to steer west by southwest when you leave Ah Ah Kaachu. That way, you'll avoid the mysterious Mists of Moro."

Sir Ollie stopped dead in his tracks. "The what?"

"The Mists of Moro," Elynor repeated, still with a frown.

"What're the Mists of Moro?" Sir Seth suddenly wanted to know.

She looked nervously at him. "No one knows. They hang over the countryside on the other side of Mount Betty like a huge see-through shroud. And whoever goes in there, never comes out."

Sir Ollie looked excitedly at Sir Seth. "Hey, Sir Seth, that sounds like something to do on the way home."

He put his hand on his sword. "Come on, Mighty Knights. Let's ride!"

Even Shasta wagged her approval.

Looking for more noble knightly adventures?

Check out the rest of the Sir Seth Thistlethwaite series from Owlkids Books!

Book One:
Sir Seth Thistlethwaite and the Soothsayer's Shoes

With the help of a saber-toothed sloth and a 3,000-year-old ghost king, Sir Seth and Sir Ollie face off against the poxy Prince Quincy of Poxley.

Book Two:
Sir Seth Thistlethwaite and the Kingdom of the Caves

Deep underground in the lost world of Claire, an ugly ogre named Ooz and his pet dino, Grak, want everything for themselves. It's up to the Mighty Knights to save the caves!

For more great books, go to:
www.owlkidsbooks.com

"There is a kid in all of us. I hope 'Sir Seth' helps you find the kid in you—and when you do, I hope you enjoy it as much as I do."

Richard Thake

Richard began his writing career at Maclean-Hunter Publishing Company in Toronto in 1958. He later moved into the advertising business, creating award-winning campaigns for many well-known corporations, and became the associate creative director of one of Canada's largest advertising agencies. A father of three grown children and a grandfather of three, Richard has finally found the time to write the Sir Seth series—a thinly disguised glimpse into his own "theater of the mind" childhood adventures with his friends in the Don River Valley and the Beach areas of Toronto.

Vince Chui

Vince has spent the last six years creating illustrations and concept artwork for various entertainment properties. While at Pseudo Interactive, he worked on Xbox 360, PlayStation 3, and PS2 games. Since then, he's moved on to do work with other industry staples, including Sega and Paramount Pictures. He enjoys character design—when he's not out playing Ultimate Frisbee.

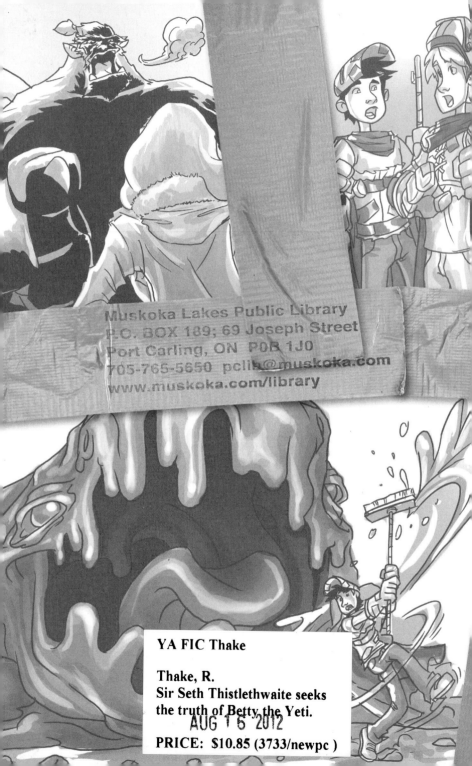